BLOODY KNUCKLES 2

BORN TO FIGHT. GROOMED TO WIN

Copyright © 2024 Tranay Adams/ BLOODY KNUCKLES 2

Published by Dope Readz Presents

All rights reserved. No part of this book may be reproduced in any form without the written consent of the publisher, except for brief quotes used in reviews.

This is a work of fiction. Any references or similarities to actual events, real people, living or dead, or real locals are intended to give the novel a sense of reality. Any similarity in other names, characters, places, and incidents is entirely coincidental.

BLOODY KNUCKLES 2
A Novel by *Tranay Adams*

Table of Contents

Chapter One 1

Chapter Two 11

Chapter Three 21

Chapter Four 32

Chapter Five 41

Chapter Six 50

Chapter Seven 61

Chapter Eight 71

Chapter Nine 80

Chapter Ten 91

Chapter Eleven 101

Chapter Twelve 112

Chapter Thirteen 122

Chapter Fourteen 132

Chapter Fifteen 144

Chapter Sixteen 154

Chapter Seventeen 164

Chapter Eighteen 173

Chapter Nineteen 180

CHAPTER ONE

Bartise's Maybach drove up to a dilapidated building with graffiti on its exterior. Its weathered appearance was a polar opposite to the vibrant energy pulsating within its walls. Purp slid out of the luxury vehicle and opened the back door for his boss. Bartise, with the assistance of his platinum cobra head cane, stepped from the backseat of his pricey whip onto the cracked pavement. He got one hell of an adrenaline rush. This was the moment he'd been waiting for—the chance to find a fighter to take him to the top.

"Fuck is Stutter, man?" Bartise frowned.

"That nigga in the front sleep, drooling like a fuckin' retard," Purp glanced back at Stutter-Box, shaking his head.

Bartise tapped Purp. "Come on. Let's get up in here."

Purp stood beside Bartise as he rapped on the old iron door of the gym. The eye-slot slid open and exposed a pair of shifty eyes. The eyes looked at Purp and then Bartise before the eye-slot closed. Bartise produced a small wad of cash with a rubber band around it. He placed it on a small tray at the center of the door. A slot behind the small tray opened and a hand picked up the money. A minute later, the locks of the iron door were undone and its latch was lifted. A fifty-six-year-old, Italian white man wearing an apple jack and chewing tobacco opened the door. When Bartise and Purp crossed the threshold it was like entering a different world.

The sounds of men training filled the air, mingling with the shouts and grunts of fighters pushing themselves to the limit. The gym was packed with fighters, each honing their skills with fierce determination.

"You see ya man in here?" Purp asked, staring at two men sparring.

"Nah. I don't think so," Bartise replied, looking around the gym. "It's beena while since I seen the kid in action. He could look completely different than what I last remembered."

A chaotic clash of noises drew Bartise and Purp's attention. They ran across the gym with several other fighters and vanished inside the locker room. The atmosphere was electric. Fighters crowded around, cheering and jeering as two men grappled violently on the tiled floor. One was a muscled man with wild, untamed hair and a ferocious look in his eyes. The other was a tall, imposing Nigerian man, his face marked with tribal scars that gave him a fearsome appearance.

"Wild Child…The legend," Bartise whispered, recognizing the man with the wild hair.

The fighters in the locker room roared as Wild Child landed a brutal punch to the Nigerian man's midsection, doubling him over. Without hesitation, he followed up with a swift uppercut, sending his opponent slamming against the lockers.

"Finish 'em, Wild Child!" one of the onlookers shouted, clutching a handful of crumpled bills. "I gotta hunnit bucks ridin' on ya!"

With a final, thunderous blow, Wild Child knocked the Nigerian man to the floor, where he lay defeated, breathing heavily and barely conscious. The locker room erupted in cheers as the gamblers collected their winnings, clapping Wild Child on the back and praising his victory.

"The kid's got something special, something real special," Bartise said, impressed with how well Wild Child handled himself.

Purp nodded. "Son got hands."

Bartise noticed a man who fit the description that his old buddy Liverowitz had given him. If his memory served him correctly the gentleman he was looking at went by Delroy Clemons. He was Wild Child's trainer and handler.

Delroy smiled as he held out his fedora, collecting his winnings from the losers as they walked past him, dropping the bets they had placed. Delroy took the money out of his hat and straightened it. He then adjusted his hat on his head and started counting the bread he'd won.

Bartise, grinning, approached Delroy with his hand extended. "How're you doing? You must be Clemons. I'm Bartise and this is Purp, my confidant."

Delroy gave Wild Child his cut from the fight. He wore a serious look on his face as he shook Bartise and then Purp's hand. "Please. Call me Delroy." Purp couldn't help noticing how much Delroy looked like Morgan Freeman. The only difference was that he wore a graying afro with the sides tapered. His dress style was like the gangsters from Bumpy Johnson's era.

"Wild Child, huh? That's an impressive fighter you got there," Bartise remarked, tone tinged with admiration.

"Kid's the best I've ever trained," Delroy replied gruffly, his voice rough from years of shouting instructions from the sidelines.

Bartise nodded, keeping his gaze on Wild Child as he approached. "Good. 'Cause I'm most definitely interested in purchasing 'em."

Wild Child walked up wiping his sweaty face with a towel. Delroy introduced him to Bartise and Purp. Wild Child nodded in greeting.

"Quite a show you put on out there," Bartise complimented his performance.

Wild Child threw the towel over his shoulder. "I take it you're who Liverowitz okayed to drop by and check me out," Bartise nodded. "Well, if you're looking for the best, you've found 'em."

"Oh, I don't doubt it," Bartise grinned.

Keeping his eyes on Wild Child, Purp whispered in Bartise's ear. "This is one cocky ass muthafucka, bruh."

"And rightfully so," Bartise whispered back. "Listen, Delroy, why don't you take a walk with me? I'd like to know a lil' bit about cha boy's background. Cool?"

"Sure."

"Purp, assist Wild Child with his training, see what he could use work on," Bartise said over his shoulder, as he walked out of the locker room beside Delroy.

Bartise listened closely as Delroy told him something only a few people knew about Wild Child. The young man's origin was one of both tragedy and brutal design. His parents, two legendary fighters, were kidnapped and taken to a remote, nondescript location. They were forced into a grotesque breeding program to produce the ultimate fighters. The resulting hybrid children were auctioned off to the highest bidders, like Africans at a slave auction.

***

The fight tournament had been a spectacle of sweat, blood, and cheers, with Luka and LaDecia emerging as the undisputed champions. The crowd's roar still echoed in their ears when, without warning, tranquilizer darts struck their necks. The potent sedative acted instantly, plunging them into darkness. Masked men swiftly moved in, handcuffing their wrists, gagging them, and duct-taping potato sacks over their heads. They were dumped into the back of an old, rusted fruit truck, its stench of decayed produce blending with the musty smell of the sacks.

The journey was a blur, a mixture of jostling movements and muffled sounds. When the truck finally stopped, Luka and LaDecia were yanked out, their gags removed, and the sacks ripped off. The harsh Brazilian sunlight made them squint, their eyes adjusting to the bright, verdant surroundings. They found themselves in front of a sprawling plantation-style house, isolated in the thick jungle. The air was humid, filled with the sounds of distant wildlife.

A slim, dark-skinned man stood on the porch, his rifle casually slung over his shoulder. He wore a large hat and suspenders, and a toothpick dangled from the corner of his mouth, twitching as he scrutinized them with hawk-like eyes. Beside him, lounging in a chair, was Demonte Rothsmith. He was a stocky man, five foot ten, with a shaved head and six-day-old stubble. His shirt was open, revealing a nest of chest hair and gold necklaces. A hyena cub gnawed on a rotten steak at his feet, its growls were a disturbing counterpoint to the serene surroundings.

Demonte looked up, his gaze as cold as the iceberg that sunk the Titanic. "Welcome to my humble abode," he said, voice dripping with mockery. "You two have been brought here because you are recognized as two of the greatest fighters in the world."

Luka and LaDecia exchanged wary glances. LaDecia spoke first, voice tinged with defiance. "What do you want with us?"

Demonte's smile was chilling. "I want you to fuck like rabbits and produce children. With your genetics, you'll create remarkable fighters. I'll sell them and make a fortune."

"So you want to breed us like dogs?" LaDecia's voice was a mix of outrage and disbelief, anger etched across her face.

"Yes," Demonte replied, his tone matter-of-fact. "And if you don't do as I ask, or if you even try to escape, you'll be shot down *just like one. Do I make myself clear?"* He looked from LaDecia to Luka, eyes daring them to defy him.

Luka's jaw tightened, and LaDecia's fists clenched at her sides, but they both knew the futility of resistance. They reluctantly nodded, their defiance momentarily subdued by the cold reality of their situation.

"Good," Demonte said, leaning back with a satisfied grin. "Now, let's get you settled in. You have a lot of work ahead of you."

As they were led inside the imposing house, Luka and LaDecia's senses were assaulted by the stark contrast between the lush exterior and the grim interior. The grand façade gave way to a hallway that felt more like a high-security prison than a home. Heavy iron doors lined the corridor, equipped with a small, barred window. The walls were painted a dull gray, and the floors were bare concrete.

Demonte led them to a room that looked exactly like a prison cell. The bed was a narrow metal cot with a thin, worn mattress. A single metal toilet stood in the corner, devoid of any privacy. The fluorescent lights buzzed overhead, casting a cold, clinical light over the bleak space.

"This will be your new home," Demonte said with a sweeping gesture, "Get comfortable."

LaDecia glared at him. "Comfortable? In this place? You've gotta be kidding."

Demonte's smile never wavered. *"Oh, I'm quite serious. You'll find that your accommodations are quite... functional."*

Luka stepped forward, his eyes locked on Demonte. *"You think you can keep us here? Treat us like animals?"*

Demonte's expression darkened. *"I don't think. Mothafucka, I know. Remember what I said: try to escape, and you will be shot down. Make no mistake about it."*

As they were led back outside, Luka and LaDecia's eyes adjusted again to the bright sunlight. The same slim man with the rifle watched them intently, his toothpick moving rhythmically as he sized them up.

On the porch, a few other men lounged, their eyes never leaving the new arrivals. They were armed with assault rifles and holding the leashes of German Shepherds.

Demonte whistled sharply for Luka and LaDecia's attention. They turned around to him holding the same hyena he had on the porch when they arrived by the fur on its neck. The cub, confused, looked around whimpering.

"In case you were wondering about these gates here," Demonte tossed the cub at the gate. It ran away hollering, having been zapped by the gate. *"They're surging with enough juice to barbeque your asses."*

Luka and LaDecia realized then that escape would be nearly impossible, surrounded by so many watchful eyes. They submitted to Demonte's demands and produced a total of seventeen *children. The only good thing that came out of their incarceration was the love they developed for each other, and the affinity they had for their children.*

***

Wild Child was one of Luka and LaDecia's hybrid offspring. He was purchased by millionaire Steven Liverowitz, known in the underground circles as a ruthless collector of human "assets." Liverowitz saw in Wild Child the potential for a living lethal weapon, a fighter unmatched on every level. To ensure the young man's savage edge, Liverowitz handed him over to Delroy Clemons, a former mercenary turned trainer.

Delroy, a man as brutal as the environment he created, raised Wild Child in conditions mimicking the harshest jungles, forcing him to live and eat like an animal, hunting and foraging to survive. This brutal lifestyle preserved his raw ferocity, making him a terrifying opponent in any fight.

Years passed, and Wild Child's reputation grew in the underground fighting circuits. His skill in hand-to-hand combat was second to none, and his savagery couldn't be contained. It wasn't long before Bartise heard of him. Acknowledging the potential, power, and profit Wild Child could bring, Bartise decided to make a move.

CHAPTER TWO

Bartise was eager to purchase Wild Child. So that night he set a date and time to meet Liverowitz to discuss a fair price.

Bartise entered the estate of Steven Liverowitz, its grandeur greatly different from the brutal world from which Wild Child came. Liverowitz's British butler opened the mansion's front door and formally welcomed him. The middle-aged servant offered Bartise something to drink and eat, but he declined. So he escorted him to the living room where the old man was relaxing. Liverowitz, who watched the burning logs in his fireplace from his wheelchair, greeted Bartise and Purp with a sly smile once his butler announced them.

"Bartise, my old friend, it's a pleasure to see you again," Liverowitz said, extending his vein-riddled, wrinkled hand.

"I'm here to talk about Wild Child," Bartise replied, cutting to the chase. "I've heard enough to know he's exactly what I need. Let's discuss terms."

Liverowitz's smile widened. "Ah, Wild Child. He's quite the specimen, isn't he? Trained to perfection by Delroy Clemons himself. But he's not cheap, you understand?"

Bartise nodded, unphased. "I understand. Name your price."

Liverowitz leaned back, contemplating. "2.5 million dollars."

"2 mill," Bartise countered with a firm tone. "And I'll make the transfer right now."

Liverowitz pretended to think it over, though both men knew he would agree. "Alright, Bartise. Two million it is. Wild Child is yours."

Bartise made the transfer, and within minutes, the deal was sealed. An hour later, Delroy Clemons and Wild Child entered the room. The young fighter's presence was almost primal, his eyes scanning Bartise with curiosity. Bartise, for the first time, took a good look at the young man. He stood six-foot-one with a middleweight boxer's physique, honey-brown eyes, and long messy hair. The name he'd been given—Wild Child—fit him to a T.

"You ready to go?" Bartise asked.

Wild Child slowly nodded. "Yeah."

As they left Liverowitz's estate, Bartise felt a surge of satisfaction. He had just acquired the most formidable fighter in the underground circuit. With Wild Child by his side, there was no telling what heights they could reach.

Delroy took Wild Child's luggage. Together, they walked through the grand mansion's corridors, the silence between them filled with unspoken words. The morning sun cast long shadows as they stepped outside, the bright light almost harsh compared to the dim interior they left behind.

Bartise's black Escalade sat in the driveway, its polished surface reflecting the early light. It was an imposing vehicle, a symbol of the change that was about to take place. Delroy and Wild Child placed the luggage into the open hatch, and Delroy slammed it shut.

Delroy turned to Wild Child, his hands moving to smooth out the wrinkles in Wild Child's suit and adjust his collar. His fingers trembled slightly, betraying the emotions he struggled to contain. Wild Child looked up at him, noticing the conflict in Delroy's usually stoic eyes.

"Delroy…" Wild Child began, his voice trailing off as he searched for the right words. But none came.

Delroy cleared his throat, his voice rough with emotion. "You've got this, kid. Remember everything I taught you."

Wild Child nodded, swallowing hard. "I won't let you down."

For a moment, they stood there in silence. Wild Child thought he saw a flicker of tears in Delroy's eyes, it was a sight so rare it almost felt like a mirage. Delroy had always been a tough, emotionless mentor, never one to show vulnerability.

Delroy reached into his pocket and pulled out a small gold rope chain with two vein-riddled fists as a charm. The chain was delicate, the gold glinted in the sunlight. He held it out to Wild Child and closed his hand around it before he could see it.

"I want you to have this," Delroy said barely above a whisper. "The fists stand for strength and resilience. You've got both in you, son."

Wild Child felt the weight of the chain in his hand, and it was a comforting presence. He looked at Delroy, the unspoken bond between them was stronger than ever.

"Thanks, Del," Wild Child said, his voice thick with emotion.

The awkwardness reached its peak as they leaned in for a hug. It was stiff and uncertain but filled with a lifetime of unspoken affection. They pulled apart, Delroy's hands lingering on Wild Child's shoulders for a moment longer.

"Take care of yourself," Delroy said. His voice was steady but his eyes betrayed the sorrow he felt.

Wild Child nodded again, eyes stinging with unshed tears. "You too, old man."

With a final nod, Wild Child climbed into the Escalade and Delroy shut the door behind him. The door closed with a heavy thud that echoed in the quiet morning. Delroy stepped back, watching as the vehicle resurrected and began to drive away.

***

In the backseat of the Escalade, Wild Child stared down at the small gold rope chain with the charm of two vein-riddled fists in his palm. He smirked as he thought about the significance of the gift given to him. For the first time in a long time, his eyes became glassy. He wiped the wetness from the corner of his eyes and slipped the chain inside his pocket.

***

Delroy stood in the driveway, a solitary figure against the backdrop of the grand mansion, his hands clenched into fists at his sides. He watched as the Escalade drove down the long driveway until it was a dot on the horizon. For the first time in years, a single tear escaped his eye and traced a path down his weathered cheek. He wiped it away quickly, taking a deep breath to steady himself. The weight of goodbye settled heavily on his shoulders, a burden he knew he would carry for a long time.

The drive back to Bartise's base was silent but charged with anticipation. Wild Child's eyes constantly scanned his surroundings, his body coiled like a spring ready to unleash its power. Bartise glanced at him through the rearview mirror, noting the tension in his new fighter's posture.

"How long have you been with the old man?" Bartise asked, breaking the silence.

"For as long as I can remember," Wild Child replied, his voice a mix of bitterness and pride. "He and Clemons made sure I never forgot what I am."

Bartise frowned with curiosity. "And what's that?"

"Something to be feared." Wild Child's eyes met Bartise's in the mirror, challenging and searching.

Bartise nodded. "Good. Fear can be a powerful weapon, but I need more than that. I need control and strategy. Can you handle that?"

Wild Child gave him a feral grin that showed a hint of his untamed spirit. "Try me."

***

Bartise gave Wild Child a tour of his enormous estate. Although anyone else would have been fascinated by the mansion, the brawler wasn't impressed in the slightest. He came from money. Liverowitz was filthy rich, and on top of that, he was powerful. The circles he was in had men and women who were caked up too. They had connections and influence. So Wild Child had seen everything a nigga could imagine to buy, from jets, planes, automobiles, villas, exotic pets, the finest of women, and even men. So while Bartise thought he was blowing his mind by showing him his plush mansion, he wasn't doing anything, besides delaying his shower and sleep.

"Now, I'll show you to your sleepin' quarters, follow me," Bartise motioned for him to follow with the hand he had his vape pen in. Stopping at the basement door, he punched in a combination code on the digital door panel beside the door. There was a metallic click. He turned the door's handle and pushed it open. He then stood aside and swayed his hand for Wild Child to enter.

"Go ahead," Bartise said, before taking another hit of his vape pen. Wild Child entered the basement and started down the staircase. The staircase was dark, and so was the basement, save for the light shining somewhere out of sight. Wild Child had walked halfway down the staircase with his luggage when he heard the basement door slam shut and lock behind him. He glanced over his shoulder and Bartise had vanished. Thinking nothing of it, he continued down the staircase until he reached the landing. He scanned his surroundings as he walked to the center of the floor. There wasn't any place for him to sit or lay. The basement was void of furniture. There was only a wall-to-wall cement floor.

"What the hell is this?" Wild Child asked under his breath.

As if on cue, a voice rang out from one of the four dark corners of the basement. "Your wake."

Wild Child looked to where the voice came from, and a rotund, five-foot-eleven white dude emerged from the shadowy corner, cracking his big, hairy knuckles. He wore a black leather vest and had bandages wrapped around his wrists.

Hearing movement over his shoulder, Wild Child's head snapped in the direction he heard shuffling. A six-foot-five man with a long ponytail emerged from a second corner, clad in a tight white t-shirt and blue jeans. He bounced around shadowboxing, kicking, and swinging his long legs. The shiny metal spurs of his cowboy boots clanged every time he brought his foot down. An old Asian fellow, in a black Kung Fu Mandarin collar frog-button shirt, cartwheeled out of a third corner, showing off his hand speed and footwork. Out of the final corner, a five-foot-nine east Indian man in a turban and traditional garb appeared, drawing a sikh rajput sword with a zoomorphic katori hilt from his side. Scowling, he gave a presentation of his skillset with the decorated blade, swiping this way and that way.

With a suitcase in each hand, Wild Child turned around in circles taking in all the men that aimed to snatch him from existence. The dangerous men charged him at the same time. Swiftly, Wild Child clobbered the Indian over the head with his suitcase, knocked homeboy with the ponytail across the face with the other, and launched it at the rotund dude's chest, dropping him. The Asian fellow leaped at Wild Child and kicked him in the chest. The Asian dude rocketed across the basement, smacking against the wall, and landing on his face. Wincing, he looked at Wild Child, got up, and charged him. Wild Child jumped up and kicked the light dangling from the ceiling. The bulb exploded and cloaked the basement in complete darkness. The sounds of fists and feet striking bodies, meshed with men hollering in agony and grunting in pain. The noise coming from the basement was loud and harsh. It stopped just as fast as it occurred.

***

Bartise, Purp, and Stutter-Box stood outside the basement door. Bartise, having grown restless, glanced at his timepiece and unlocked the basement door. Looking down from the top step, he made note of the basement being pitch-black and silent. He called out the names of the men he'd hired to do a number on Wild Child, and even Wild Child himself but he didn't receive a reply.

"What—what—what chu thank happened dow—down there?" Stutter-Box asked no one specifically.

Purp shrugged. "I don't know, Stutter, but let's find out," he drew his gun from the front of his jeans, and Stutter-Box mimicked his action. "You gotta flashlight, boss dawg?"

"No. But I do have a cellphone," Bartise tucked away his vape pen and pulled out his cellular. He activated its flashlight option and motioned for Purp and Stutter-Box to follow him inside the basement. The men carefully walked down the staircase, listening to their boss call out the names of the thugs he'd employed.

"Boogaloo? Towl? Cardone? Krishna?" Bartise called for his henchmen's attention. An eerily silence remained, leaving him wondering what he was about to find inside the basement.

CHAPTER THREE

"You—you—you think, Wil—Wild Child clean—cleaned them niggaz up?" Stutter-Box asked from beside Purp. Their guns were gripped and extended before them like a couple of cops, approaching a hostile situation.

"Hell naw. I know he's supposed to be this great, big Billy Bad Ass muthafucka, but he's not superhuman," Purp replied, keeping his eyes on what was in front of him. "Bartise dropped a nice sum of dough on these fools. They're supposed to be some of the coldest dudes from their parts of the map."

"I—I don't know, kid. Wild—Wild Child was—was born to—to fight and—and groomed to win." Stutter-Box reasoned.

Purp frowned and sucked his teeth. "Yo, son, let go of this nigga's meat."

"You—you—you can kiss my—my bl—black ass." Stutter-Box retorted.

"Holy shit." Purp's eyes bubbled, mouth hanging open.

Stutter-Box tried to say something but his words got caught in his throat.

A smile slowly formed on Bartise's lips as he held his flashlight on the sight before him. Wild Child, who was bloody at the mouth and hair, had his foot planted on a dead Boogaloo's belly. In one hand, he held Krishna by the collar as he lay limp on the floor. His head was twisted completely to his back and his suffering was written on his face. In his other hand, he held Cardone by his face like a bowling ball. Two of his fingers were in his eye sockets, down to their knuckles and his thumb was pressed against the roof of his mouth. In the background, Towl hung from the wall, impaled by Krishna's sikh rajput sword.

"Wild Child. Yeaaah. That's what I'm talkin' about, baby." Bartise looked at Wild Child like he was a chest full of gold he'd just opened. "Purp. Stutter-Box. Y'all clean this mess up, while I show my guest to his room." Bartise passed Purp his flashlight, picked up Wild Child's luggage, and motioned with his head for him to follow him up the staircase.

Wild Child wiped his bloody hands on Cardone's shirt and stepped over Krishna's body, following Bartise up the staircase.

Bartise stood at the bottom of the staircase watching Wild Child's back as he climbed the steps. He looked at Stutter-Box who was struggling to drag Boogaloo toward the staircase. "Son, that nigga's nutty as a goddamn Payday. His beastly ass needa be set free in the wild or something."

***

Bartise showed Wild Child his bedroom and he went straight to the bathroom. He stripped naked, fixed the temperature of the shower water to his liking, and stepped into the tub. The hot shower water rinsed away the blood and the steam enveloped him like a superhero's cape. He stood there for a long moment, letting the water cleanse not just his body, but his mind.

Wild Child emerged from the bathroom glistening wet, tying his bathrobe around his waist. His long, damp hair clung to his back, and he felt a rare moment of calm. But the calm was quickly replaced by surprise when he noticed a cart in the middle of his bedroom. A shiny gold platter with a matching bubble top lid and an expensive bottle of champagne nestled in a bucket of ice awaited him. Curious, he approached the cart. The bottle of champagne caught his eye first. He grabbed it, feeling the cold glass against his skin. With a practiced motion, he popped the cork and guzzled the champagne, bubbles tickling his throat and sliding down his chin. He set the bottle down and lifted the lid off the platter, revealing a feast fit for a king: two medium-rare tomahawk steaks, a three-pound lobster, a loaded baked potato, and broccoli. Wild Child didn't hesitate. He dug into the meal with gusto, savoring the rich flavors. It was a far cry from the bland, utilitarian food he'd grown accustomed to. Each bite was a revelation, and for a moment, he allowed himself to forget the brutality of his life. When he finished, he belched contentedly and wiped his mouth with a cloth napkin.

    Wild Child moved to his suitcase and took out a pair of boxer briefs, pulling them up on his waist. He was about to slip on his wife beater when a knock on the door made him pause. His forehead wrinkled wondering who it could be, walking across his bedroom and opening the door. Wild Child's breath caught in his throat. Standing before him were two stunning women, their balloon-sized breasts barely contained by their matching black bikini tops. They licked their perfect white teeth and stared at him with a hunger that made his pulse quicken. Wild Child felt a surge of lust. Although he was twenty-five, he had never been with a woman before. He had been bred to fight, trained day in and day out with no time for anything else. But he was still a young man with sexual wants, needs, and urges. He promised himself that tonight would be the night he'd find out what it was like to be with a woman.

"Who...who are y'all?" Wild Child stammered, trying not to sound nervous, eyes wide with curiosity and desire.

The taller of the two women's lips curled into a sultry smile that made his heart race. "We're here to help you relax," she purred, stepping closer and caressing his face. "From what Bartise told us, you've earned it."

The other woman nodded, eyes sweeping over his body. "Yeah. Let us take care of you."

The women entered the room, their hands trailing over Wild Child's scarred body, their lips pressing tender kisses to his skin. He felt a shiver run down his back as they caressed his pecs and six-pack abs. Just as he began to lose himself in the sensations, the door opened again.

Bartise walked in, a broad smile on his face. "Enjoying yourself?" he asked, eyes twinkling with amusement.

Wild Child nodded, still overwhelmed by the sensations coursing through him. "What's all this about?"

Bartise clapped him on the shoulder. "This is about fulfilling your fantasies. Now, tell me, what do you want?"

Without hesitation, Wild Child replied, "I want to see my family. I want to meet my parents."

Wild Child had tried to make a deal with Liverowitz to meet his parents, but he gave him the runaround. When he pressed the issue further, the old man threatened to chop off one of his feet like Kunta Kinte. The fear of having one of his feet severed spooked Wild Child and he never brought up the idea of meeting his folks again.

Bartise's smile faltered slightly, but he quickly recovered. "I can't promise you that, unless you crush these fights I have lined up for you."

Wild Child nodded again, and they shook hands. Bartise placed a gold foil Magnum condom on the bed and left the room, closing the door.

Left alone with the women, Wild Child allowed himself to indulge in his desires, experiencing pleasures he had only imagined.

***

Wild Child slipped out of bed, leaving the two women he'd slept with. The early morning light shone through the curtains, casting a soft glow on the room. He stood before his nightstand mirror and took in his appearance. His face, body, and knuckles bore the scars from countless fights, both in and out of the ring. Each scar told a story of triumph and victory, which he was proud of, and wore with pride. He was a warrior, and his battles had forged him like a blacksmith forging hot metal into a sword.

Reaching inside his nightstand drawer, Wild Child retrieved the gold rope chain with the vein-riddled fist charm that Delroy had given him. He clasped it around his neck, adjusting the chain so the charm lay against his chest. As soon as he touched it, memories of fights with Delroy Clemons by his side flashed through his mind like a series of movie scenes. He was so engrossed in his past experiences that he didn't notice one of the women from last night picking through his hair, running her fingers gently through it.

"Your hair's a mess," she murmured, her voice soft and playful. "Lemme braid it for you."

Wild Child glanced at her in the mirror and nodded, a small smile playing on his lips. "Sure, why not?"

She slipped into one of his undershirts and her bikini bottoms, then grabbed a rat-tail comb and a jar of Vaseline. Sitting at the end of the bed, she patted the space between her thighs and motioned for him to sit down. Wild Child settled himself between her legs, resting the side of his head against her thigh. She began to part and braid his hair, singing softly as she worked.

As her fingers moved deftly through his hair, he closed his eyes and imagined she was his mother, holding him as a baby and singing to him. He didn't know what his mother looked like, but long ago he had created an image of her in his mind. Her touch was soothing, and for a moment, he allowed himself to be transported to a place of comfort and security.

When she finished braiding, Wild Child opened his eyes and looked in the mirror. The cornrows were tight and neat, giving him a fresh, fierce look. He turned his head from side to side, admiring the work.

"Thank you," he said, voice filled with genuine appreciation.

She smiled, pleased with his reaction. "You're welcome. You look good."

By this time, the other woman, Wild Child, had sex with the night before stirred awake. She stretched and yawned, a lazy smile spreading across her face as she noticed Wild Child's new hairstyle.

"You know if you were to getta line up and trim your beard. You could do some modeling," she said.

Wild Child smirked, thinking she was on some bullshit. Though he was an attractive young man, he didn't see himself in that light.

The three of them made their way to the bathroom, where they took a shower together. The warm water cascaded over them, washing away the remnants of the previous night. They made out under the steamy spray, their passion reigniting. The shower turned into another round of fucking, their bodies moving in a rhythm as old as time.

Afterward, they dried off and returned to the bed, their skin still glistening with water. Wild Child lay back, feeling a rare sense of peace. The morning had been a blend of reflection, intimacy, and connection, a temporary escape from the brutal reality of his life.

He looked at the two women beside him, their faces relaxed and content. For a fleeting moment, he allowed himself to believe in the possibility of a different life—a life where he could find solace and joy outside of fighting. But as always, the call of the fight, the need for victory, and the thrill of the battle would pull him back.

The day ahead would bring new challenges and battles, but for now, Wild Child savored the calm. He reached for the gold necklace around his neck, feeling the reassuring weight of the charm. Delroy's voice echoed in his mind, reminding him of the warrior he was and the battles he had yet to fight.

He glanced at the women beside him, giving them a warm smile. "Let's grab some breakfast."

They laughed and agreed, their voices blending into a harmonious melody. As they got dressed and headed to the kitchen, Wild Child felt ready to face whatever the day would bring, strengthened by the memories of his past and the connections of the present.

Over the next two weeks, Wild Child fought twenty opponents, defeating each one with a combination of brute strength and skill, earning Bartise a small fortune. Each fight was a brutal testament to his training and raw power, and each victory brought him one step closer to the promise Bartise had made. His opponents ranged from seasoned veterans to up-and-coming fighters, each presenting a unique challenge. Wild Child's

BLOODY KNUCKLES 2

reputation grew with each victory, the crowds cheering louder, and the stakes growing higher.

After his twentieth victory, Bartise called a meeting with Purp and Stutter-Box. They gathered in Bartise's office, a lavish room with floor-to-ceiling windows that offered a breathtaking view of the ocean.

"I'm gonna host a fighting tournament at my estate in Bali," Bartise announced, voice leaking excitement. "No U.S. jurisdiction and we'll charge a million dollars per fighter and half a million per admission. "I'll make more money than I ever dreamed of."

Purp and Stutter-Box exchanged impressed glances, nodding in agreement. "Sounds like a brilliant plan," Purp said, a grin spreading across his lips.

Stutter-Box nodded enthusiastically. "Yeah—yeah, man, this—this is—is gonna be huge."

Bartise began to brainstorm how to send invitations to his wealthy associates, his mind already racing with possibilities for his next big score. "We'll need to make sure everything is perfect," he mused, toying with the cobra head of his cane. "The right fighters, the right audience. This could be the biggest event ever."

Purp leaned forward, eyes gleaming with excitement. "We should reach out to the top fighters worldwide. This needa be an event that no one will want to miss."

Bartise nodded. "Agreed. We'll send personal invitations to the best of the best. This tournament needs to be exclusive, something people will talk about for years."

As Bartise continued to plan, Wild Child sat back in his chair with a flicker of hope in his eyes. This could be his chance to find his family and finally understand where he came from. He listened intently as Bartise talked about logistics and marketing strategies.

Bartise looked at Wild Child and knew what was on his mind. He didn't need to say it. "Kid, you come out on top in this thang, and I'll give you what chu asked for."

"I want your word," Wild Child said sternly, rising from his chair.

Bartise rose from his chair, extending his hand. "You have my word."

They shook hands sealing the deal.

CHAPTER FOUR

Chyna sat on the bench outside D'Anthony's building with a blunt hanging from his lips. His head was on a swivel as he blew clouds of smoke and kept his right hand inside his jacket pocket. Although these same projects were once home to him and Jayvon, his parents didn't raise fools. He and his team were getting mad dough, so they looked like lambs to the wolves scouring the slums.

When Chyna saw a hooded figure walking out of D'Anthony's tenement, he could tell it was the young nigga from the bop in his walk. So he hopped off the bench and greeted him with their exclusive handshake.

"What up, kid? To what pleasure do I owe this lil' wake-up call?" D'Anthony yawned and stretched his arms. Chyna could tell from the bags under his eyes and the dry white stuff at the corner of his mouth he'd been asleep. As much as he hated to wake him up at three in the morning it was necessary, he needed someone to have his back and he was the only person he could trust.

"Son, me and bro are into some real shit. I'm talkin' waist deep," Chyna started, passing him the blunt. D'Anthony listened closely as he sucked on the end of the bleezy. Chyna gave him the entire rundown on what was up with his father Trick, and his being in the hospital. "Right now, my bro and the homies are doing everythang they gotta do to raise the money. I gotta be on my shit too, which is why I'm here right now. I need you with me to get this bag, but it's gotta be off the books, bro. Dolph and them niggaz can't know nothin' about this. I can't afford to kick up a cut to the Gods 'cause I'ma need every dolla I can get to make this five mill."

D'Anthony whistled when he heard his big homie needed five million dollars to keep his father alive. "I know, my nigga. I know. That's a lotta loot, but with all of us working together we can make this shit happen." Chyna assured him, smacking the back of his hand into his palm for emphasis.

"Say no more, big homie, you know ya boy down for the cause." D'Anthony shook up with him.

The next day

Jayvon agreed to pay Draco the five million dollars he was asking for. He understood that if he didn't make the deal his old man would be murdered right there in front of him. As soon as the Facetime between him and Draco was over, the time clock started ticking and the money had to be earned within two weeks. If Jayvon and the gang couldn't come up with it they'd have to make funeral arrangements for Trick.

Jayvon stretched his arms and legs, twisted his waist from side to side, and rolled his head around his shoulders. He moved swiftly, shadowboxing, displaying his skill set to the crowd. Suddenly, the sea of Bloods parted, revealing a mammoth of a man. The giant stood a whopping six-foot-five and weighed all two hundred and sixty-five pounds. He had a beige complexion, a gleaming bald head, and a chin like a superhero. A red bandana adorned his forehead and another tied around his neck like a cape. The massive man towered over Jayvon, shading him from the sun like a tree.

Jayvon stared up at his opponent, his stomach doing backflips. He wasn't scared, but he was nervous. He had never fought anyone this big in all his years. Bloodsport's body was covered in bulging muscles, making him look like a living, breathing tank. Jayvon sized him up, determined to find a weak spot, despite the man's imposing presence.

"What the fuck happened to the sun?" Jayvon thought, trying to calm his racing heart.

"Readyyyyyy. Setttttttt. Fight!" the referee bellowed.

Jayvon struck first with a three-punch combo, landing two blows to Bloodsport's body and finishing with an uppercut. Bloodsport brought his head back down, spat blood on the ground, and smiled, revealing bloody teeth.

"Yeaaaah. That's what I'm talkin' about," Bloodsport said, his voice dripping with excitement. He cocked back his boxing glove-sized fist and swung forward with all his might.

Bag Man, Augustus, and Chyna cringed as the punch connected, sending Jayvon hurling backward. The crowd parted as he rocketed through them, slamming up against two Ducati Supersports before landing on the ground beside them. Groaning, Jayvon looked up, wincing at the sight of Bloodsport casually strolling toward him, bending his neck from side to side and winding up the same arm he'd used to punch him.

Unh, my chest is killin' me. Feels like a stick of dynamite went off inside of me, Jayvon thought, rubbing his aching chest.

"Come on, bro. You can beat this chump, show 'em how we get down for ours," Chyna shouted from the audience while filming the brawl with his cell phone.

"Yeah, youngin', up and at 'em, show his big ass what chu got," Augustus added, showing off his boxing skills and fancy footwork.

Jayvon locked eyes with Bag Man, looking for some guidance.

"Fuck you looking at me for, bitch? Get cho ass up and drop them dogs on his big ass," Bag Man barked, throwing a three-punch combination at an imaginary opponent. He swung his hand, signaling Jayvon to jump back into the fight.

"Thanks a lot, coach," Jayvon muttered under his breath, getting back up. By the time he looked, Bloodsport was charging at him like a freight train, ready to knock fire from him. At the last minute, Jayvon stepped out of the way. Bloodsport's momentum carried him forward, and he crashed to the ground, bumping the side of his head. Embarrassed, he scrambled back to his feet and threw up his fists.

"I'm gonna knock yo' head into outer space, Blood!" Bloodsport promised, seething with anger.

Jayvon approached with his fists up, ducking, dodging, and countering every punch the giant threw at him. He danced around Bloodsport, sticking and moving with agility. For every punch Bloodsport threw, Jayvon retaliated with two. Eventually, the bigger man exhausted himself, struggling to land a solid blow.

"Come on, son, don't tell me you're tired. We're just now getting started," Jayvon taunted, dancing around him.

Bloodsport looked around at the pitiful faces of those who had bet on him. The homies didn't look too proud; they looked ashamed. This realization fueled his rage. His face twisted into a mask of hatred, veins bulging across his muscular body. Summoning the last of his strength, he charged at Jayvon, determined to end the fight.

Jayvon saw the desperation in Bloodsport's eyes. He braced himself, ready to outmaneuver the giant one last time. As Bloodsport lunged, Jayvon sidestepped with a swift, fluid motion, delivering a powerful blow to Bloodsport's jaw. The impact sent a shockwave through Bloodsport's body, and he staggered, his knees buckling.

Jayvon seized the opportunity, launching a flurry of punches that connected with precision and force. Bloodsport swayed, his eyes glazing over. With a final uppercut, Jayvon sent the giant crashing to the ground, the crowd erupting in cheers.

Breathing heavily, Jayvon stood over his fallen opponent, victorious. He glanced at his friends, who were cheering and shouting their approval. Despite the bruises and the pain, Jayvon felt a surge of pride. He had faced the giant and won, proving his strength and resilience.

The fight was over, but the victory was just the beginning. Jayvon knew there were more battles ahead, but with his friends by his side and his newfound confidence, he was ready for whatever came next.

***

There was a high-stakes poker game going down in lower Manhattan. There was plenty of food, alcohol, and exclusive cigars for everyone. Money exchanged hands with the casual indifference of a lover's touch, each chip was a small emblem of power and greed in the game of chance. Wise guys, kingpins, gang officials, and even a couple of crooked cops rounded out the tables, conversing and laughing, like old college buddies.

Unbeknownst to the motley crew of players, two figures lurked in the hallway, their eyes glinted with the predatory hunger of leopards stalking antelopes. Clad in dark clothing that seemed to absorb the scant light like a black hole, they moved with the stealthy grace of panthers on the prowl.

With a silent nod of understanding, the two men sprang into action, their movements synchronized in a deadly dance of deception and intimidation. From the depths of their coats, they produced cold- steel with silencers on their barrels.

Ba-doom!

The front door flew open, startling everyone at the card tables. Augustus and Bag Man, disguised in black sunglasses and ski masks, run in shouting commands and waving their pistols.

"Bet notta muthafucka in here move 'less we tell you to," Bag Man barked.

"That's right, keep yo' hands where our eyes can see 'em. No sudden moves, or I'll pop one in yo' degenerate ass!" Augustus added. Everyone at the tables had their hands up and were mad dogging him and Bag Man.

"We only want chu bitchez' money, not your lives, so don't force us to leave with 'em both!" Bag Man said.

The players didn't like the barrels of the pistols trained on them like the eye of a vengeful god. This was the first time some of them were at the mercy of anyone and it didn't sit right with them. The ringleader of the poker game, a burly fellow with unique scars on his face and a reputation for brutality, glared defiantly at Augustus and Bag Man.

"You punks think you can just waltz in here and demand what's ours?" he spat viciously. "You've gotta 'nother thing coming."

Augustus and Bag Man looked at each other. Augustus shrugged. Bag Man popped the wise guy in his belly. He fell out of his chair, hollering like a wounded bear, holding himself.

"Anyone else got something to say?" Bag Man asked, looking around at the men at the tables. No one dared to say a word. "Y'all smart than a muthafucka in here." He whispered something into Augustus's ear, prompting him to tuck his gun at the small of his back and draw a pillowcase from his back pocket. "My partner's gonna come around to your tables. You're to place alla the money you have inside his pillowcase." he watched as Augustus made his rounds, retrieving the cash. "For you slick muthafuckaz, we want the gwap in yo' socks, yo' wallets, yo' money belts, even the bread you're hidin' under those ridiculous ass hairpieces."

The players at the tables came up off the bread from all their hiding places. A couple of men had money stashed in their hairpieces too.

In the end, Augustus and Bag Man left with a pillowcase filled with money and jewelry. The men they'd robbed were left in their boxers, gagged and zip-tied, squirming to get free.

CHAPTER FIVE

The night was dark. Cold. Still. Everything besides quiet. D'Anthony and his semi-automatic Uzi made sure of this. He was masked and hanging halfway out of the passenger window of a white, black ragtop Ford Mustang. Chyna sat in the driver's seat with determination on his face. He had one hand on the steering wheel while the other gripped the gearshift. He and D'Anthony have been on their target's ass for three blocks now. He was a hefty-nigga, weighing about two-hundred-and-fifty-six pounds, so they expected him to have tired two and a half blocks ago, but they never calculated in his will to live boosting his adrenaline.

"Haa! Haa! Haa! Haa! Haa! Haa!" Deon huffed and puffed as he fled from the blinding headlights of the speeding Mustang. He occasionally glanced over his shoulder, wiping the sweat on his forehead. "Please, God, please! I'm beggin' you."

Deon thought aloud. He'd sent a prayer up to The Almighty to send one of his angels from the heavens, to swoop him off his feet to safety. He swore on his dead granny that if the Lord pulled his chunky ass out of this one he'd become a pastor and dedicate the rest of his life to spreading HIS gospel. Unfortunately for old Deon, The Big Man in the Sky had heard this very same speech from him a million times, so he knew he was full of shit. He'd have to ride this one out alone.

Bratatatatatatat! Click, click, click!

D'Anthony's Uzi clicked empty. He checked its clip to be sure he needed to reload.

"Fuck, dawg!" D'Anthony cussed as he ducked back inside the Mustang and pulled off his ski mask. Sweat poured down his face as he grabbed a fresh clip and reloaded his stick.

Chyna glanced at D'Anthony. "You get 'em?"

"Man, hell naw. I will though. Slow this muthafucka up. I got this." D'Anthony assured him, emerging from the passenger window and sitting on the pane. As Chyna slowed the Mustang down, D'Anthony upped the Uzi and lined it up with Deon's back. The young nigga calmed down, slowing his breathing. He squeezed the semi-automatic trigger and it kicked back to life. Bullets zipped across the air, and seconds later Deon plopped into the middle of the street. "I got 'em."

D'Anthony smiled and wiped the sweat from his forehead. Once the Mustang stopped, he pulled his legs out of the car and jumped down to the pavement. Holding his Uzi up at his shoulder, he walked towards Deon like he had all the time in the world to kill him.

Bleeding at the mouth, Deon made a pathetic attempt to crawl away. He was kicking himself in the ass now for having knocked up his plug's thirteen-year-old daughter. The violation had gotten a fifteen thousand dollar bag placed on his head, and the likes of Chyna and D'Anthony on his ass.

"What the fuck is this nigga doing?" Chyna frowned, watching D'Anthony take his sweet time turning off Deon's faucet. Hearing police car sirens approaching, he glanced out of the back window and stuck his head out of the driver's side window. "My nigga, stop fuckin' around and cut that fool's water off." He hollered out to D'Anthony.

"A'ight, big homie, I gotchu," D'Anthony replied, training his Uzi on Deon. The poor bastard had just turned over to beg for his life when a spray of hot lead swept across his chest. Deon fell back to the asphalt with his arm outstretched and his head lying against it. To be sure he was dead, the youngin' gave him another spray across his chest and retreated to the Mustang. As soon as he hopped in, Chyna spun around in reverse and took off in the direction they came from.

***

"That's right, baby, kick his ass!" Chrissy shouted from behind the bandana, covering the lower half of her face. She and the audience stood on the sidelines watching Jayvon and Dirty Dan fight. Most of those in attendance were either wearing an oxygen mask, a surgical mask, or some sort of bandana, to protect them from Jayvon's opponent's stench.

Bwop, bop, wop, bwack!

Jayvon came at Dirty Dan fast and hard, connecting to his torso and face. Each blow that connected sent ripples through Dirty Dan's flesh and jaw. Dust and sweat flew from his body, but he didn't fall. When Jayvon pulled back, Dirty Dan's eyes rolled to the back of his head and he was wobbly. It was like he was just standing there, waiting for Jayvon to finish him off.

"Finish his musty ass!" Someone from the audience shouted.

"Yeah, lay his funky ass out, yo!" Someone else from the audience shouted.

"Drop 'em, baby!" Chrissy demanded, swinging her fist like she was fighting Dirty Dan.

Jayvon charged at Dirty Dan scowling and screaming. He was coming at him so fast that everything else surrounding him looked blurry. Leaping up, he cocked his fist back as far as he could, prepared to deliver the finishing blow. Upon impact, a mist of blood went in the air and Dirty Dan flew backwards. In midair, Jayvon did a 180-degree turn and landed on his back, grimacing. Seconds later, Dirty Dan fell beside him, snoring asleep and bleeding at the mouth. A few brown roaches ran out of his torn-up sweatpants and scattered across the ground. Then the mothafucka farted!

Those of the audience that betted on Jayvon jumped, cheered, and shouted his name. Chrissy bumped her way through the crowd that formed around her man. She helped him to his feet and threw his arm around her shoulders.

"Let's get outta here."

***

The warehouse echoed with the hushed whispers of Augustus and Bag Man as they watched over their captive, the son of a wealthy car dealership owner. Bound and gagged, the young man sat in a chair, eyes wide with fear as he unsuccessfully struggled to get out of his restraints.

"Youngin', if you don't stop tryna get outta those ropes, you're gonna find your brain lying on your left shoulder, ya dig?" Bag Man threatened, tapping his finger against the pistol inside his waistband. Instantly, the young man stopped moving and tears slid down his cheeks. He bowed his head and prayed to God his father came through with the money the kidnappers wanted because if he didn't, he was sure he was a dead man.

An anxious Augustus paced back and forth, his eyes fixed on the entrance. "Man, where the fuck is this dude?" he muttered, his voice tense with anticipation.

Bag Man was just as anxious as Augustus. He couldn't shake the feeling that old man Quilez was setting them up. Right then he made up his mind if old man Quilez got the F.B.I. involved, he wouldn't go quietly. Fuck that. He'd go out talking shit and busting his gun until he was eventually taken out.

Bag Man, tapping his foot impatiently, pulled back the sleeve of his jacket and checked the time on his watch. "I don't know. That cocksucka shoulda been here twenty minutes ago," he told Augustus, his voice barely above a whisper. "I made it clear that if he wants to see his kid alive, he needs to come alone with that money."

"This might sound fucked up, but if this turns into a shit show then I'm blastin' that old spic and his kid's gettin' it, too," Augustus swore, pointing his gun at the car dealership owner's son.

"There'll be no need for that," a dark figure appeared in the warehouse's entrance, holding what looked like a briefcase. "I apologize for my tardiness, but I got caught in traffic."

Augustus and Bag Man didn't bother asking who he was because they knew it was Wilmer Quilez. The sixty-two-year-old car dealer didn't wait to be invited inside. He walked inside the warehouse like his name was on the deed of it. The sound of his footsteps echoed throughout the tenement, making Augustus and Bag Man tense. Their hands instinctively tightened around the handles of their guns, and they scanned their surroundings, thinking the authorities would emerge from the shadows to arrest them. Their suspicions were put to rest when nothing of the sort happened. The old man had shown up alone like he had been told. He was dressed in a tailor-made suit and an overcoat.

Old man Quilez's face was fixed with worry, lines of stress were etched into his brows as he approached, eyes pinned on his son. "Please," he began, his voice choking with emotion. "Let my son go. I have the money, just as you requested."

Augustus took a step forward, eying the briefcase in the old man's grip. "You'll get your hier as soon as we make sure every coin of that three-hundred thousand is there," he assured Quilez, with a guttural tone. He looked at Bag Man and motioned him over to Quilez with his gun. "Pat this nigga down, hoss, make sure he isn't packin'."

"I walked in here naked, I'm not holding anything," Quilez said, holding his coat open so Augustus and Bag Man could see he didn't have a gun.

"While you may be tellin' the truth, I'm not gonna gamble on it," Augustus told him.

Bag Man tucked his gun and walked over to Quilez. He took the briefcase from him and sat it on the ground. He ordered him against the wall with his arms and legs spread. He then patted him down like he saw the police do in more movies than he cared to remember.

"Nigga clean, man," Bag Man reported. He kneeled to the briefcase, popped its locks, and lifted its lid, revealing stacks and stacks of crisp one-hundred dollar bills bound together with rubber bands. The sight seemed to satisfy him and Augustus, they exchanged a silent nod of approval.

"You got your money, now release my boy," old man Quilez said, his voice cold and emotionless.

Bag Man stood upright with the briefcase full of cash. "Youz an impatient ass nigga, pops. Nigga gon' and get cho son and get outta here." he threw his head toward his son. Old man Quilez nearly fell rushing to his son's side to untie him. He removed the gag from the boy's mouth and got to work untying the ropes that bound him. The boy nodded gratefully to his father, scrambling to his feet, eyes wide with relief as he threw himself into his arms. He shuddered as he cried against his old man's chest. Quilez kissed the side of his son's head and rubbed his back to comfort him. Quilez looked at Augustus and Bag Man's backs as they left the warehouse.

Although they were walking away with a nice chunk of cash, the money wasn't anything to a man with Quilez's riches. On top of that, that bread was nothing compared to the life of his son. He would have given them ten times that if it meant he'd get his boy back.

CHAPTER SIX

Blowl, blowl, blowl!
Blocka, blocka, blocka, blocka!

Pop, pop!

An exchange of hostile gunfire erupted inside of a stash house. Its front door flew open and Chyna and D'Anthony ran out, wearing duffle bags like backpacks. They cut through the front lawn, each clenching a warm, smoking gun and glancing over their shoulders. The two men they'd robbed appeared in the doorway armed.

"Get the car, son, I'll hold you down!" Chyna called out to D'Anthony. He then turned around and fired at one of the two men. His target took two to the chest and fell back on the porch, still holding his piece.

"Blaise!" the other man cried, seeing his homeboy chopped down. Infuriated, he set his sights on Chyna who was hauling ass up the sidewalk, a few feet away from D'Anthony. The man snarled, lifted his pole, and sent three rounds back at him.

Blocka, blocka, blocka!

The back passenger window of a Ford Taurus exploded as Chyna ran past it. Its side view mirror came apart next. A third bullet zipped through Chyna's duffel bag and left a hole behind. Looking ahead, he saw the backlights of the getaway car come on as its engine came to life. He snatched open the front passenger door and hopped in. D'Anthony opened the driver's door, hopped out, and aimed his pole over the vehicle's roof. He squeezed its trigger relentlessly. The first bullet slammed into the gunman's belly. The next one hit him high in the chest. Another hit him directly in the forehead while the last one zipped through his neck. He fell on the porch and tumbled down the steps of the house, losing his gun. D'Anthony hopped behind the wheel of the getaway car, shifted it into drive, and peeled away without looking in the review mirror for oncoming traffic.

The lights of houses on both sides of the street began popping on. The dogs started barking. The sounds of police car sirens wailed loudly.

***

The old high school lunch room, once a place of mundane chatter and cafeteria food, had been transformed into a battleground. The dust-covered tables and broken benches surrounded the makeshift ring where Jayvon and Enoch faced off. The crowd, packed tightly and buzzing with anticipation, roared as the two fighters circled each other. The atmosphere was electric, the air thick with tension and excitement.

Jayvon moved with agility, his fists up and eyes locked on Enoch. The fight was evenly matched, each punch and counter-punch a testament to their skill and determination. The crowd cheered with every landed blow, their voices rising in a cacophony of encouragement.

Enoch, a powerful and ruthless fighter, began to gain the upper hand. His punches came faster and harder, and Jayvon struggled to keep up. A brutal punch to Jayvon's head made his vision blur. He felt dizzy as if he was experiencing vertigo, and his balance faltered. He fell to his hands and knees, struggling to steady himself.

The crowd's cheers grew louder as Enoch saw his opportunity. He charged at Jayvon, eyes filled with a wicked gleam. Jayvon saw him coming but couldn't react in time. Enoch's foot connected with his head, sending him sprawling onto his back.

Enoch climbed onto a dusty lunch table, grinning wickedly as he prepared for his finishing move. The crowd hyped him up, chanting his name. He smacked his elbow twice, signaling The Dead Drop, his signature move. The crowd's anticipation reached a fever pitch as Enoch launched himself off the table.

At the last possible moment, Jayvon threw up his foot. Enoch's momentum carried him directly onto it, his balls taking the full impact. Enoch's face contorted in agony as he fell to the ground, clutching himself and fighting back tears.

Seizing the opportunity, Jayvon crawled over to Enoch and locked him in a chokehold. Enoch thrashed and squirmed, trying desperately to free himself, but Jayvon's grip was too strong. Enoch's breaths came in short, panicked gasps as he struggled to breathe. Unable to endure the chokehold any longer, Enoch tapped out, signaling his defeat.

The referee rushed in, raising Jayvon's hand in victory. The crowd erupted in cheers, their excitement reaching a crescendo. Jayvon scrambled to his feet, but the room spun around him. His vision blurred and he swayed unsteadily, barely able to keep his balance.

Chrissy, who had been watching anxiously from the sidelines, ran out and caught him before he could fall. "I've got you," she said, her voice steady and reassuring despite the chaos around them.

The referee called out, "Your winner, Bllllloodyyyy Knuuuucklllles!" The crowd's cheers grew louder, echoing through the dilapidated lunch room.

Jayvon, supported by Chrissy, raised his hand in a gesture of triumph. Despite the pain and the dizziness, a smile spread across his face. He had won, against all odds. The crowd's cheers filled his ears, a testament to his hard-fought victory.

Chrissy slipped Jayvon's arm around her shoulders as they walked toward the exit. A few fans approached Jayvon giving him props on his latest victory and requesting pictures. Feeling woozy, he respectfully declined any pictures, but he did autograph some merchandise. He was in the middle of signing a couple of teenagers' graphic t-shirts with his image on them when the room began shaking and tilting. The Sharpie marker slipped out of his hand. He blinked his eyes repeatedly and his legs buckled. Everyone stared at him with bizarre looks, wondering what was wrong.

"Von, what's wrong?" Chrissy panicked, reaching out for him.

"Babe, I don't—I don't—" Jayvon tried to grab Chrissy's hand but missed, taking a fall. He hit the pavement hard, lying on his back and watching his world spin.

"Oh, my God, someone call 9-1-1!" Chrissy shouted, getting on the ground and resting Jayvon's head in her lap. She tried talking to him, but everything he said came out gibberish. "Hold on, baby! Please, hold on!" she cried.

Chrissy's voice was the last one Jayvon heard before darkness claimed him.

***

An ambulance with its emergency siren and light blaring flew up the street. Cars drove to the opposite side of the road and gave the transporting vehicle a wide berth. It zipped through red lights and intersections.

***

In the dimly lit examination room, the weight of silence hung thick as Jayvon anxiously awaited the doctor's verdict. The air seemed to have been charged with uncertainty as the doctor carefully reviewed the MRI scans. Jayvon, a seasoned fighter, had faced countless opponents, each blow a testament to his resilience. Little did he know, the true battle lay within his mind.

The doctor finally broke the silence, his expression grave. "Jayvon, I'm afraid I have difficult news. The repeated blows to your head have led to a condition known as Cavum septum pellucidum. It's a form of brain damage, and one more severe impact could prove fatal, or permanently blind you. I strongly advise you to reconsider your career in fighting."

Staring at the doctor in disbelief, Jayvon felt the gravity of the words sinking into his brain. The very thing that defined him, that gave him purpose and identity, was now a danger to his own life. The room seemed to close in on him, the walls echoing the harsh reality of his situation.

Outside the examination room, Chrissy nervously paced the corridor. As the door opened, she looked into Jayvon's eyes, searching for answers. The weight of the news was etched across his face.

Chrissy pleaded, her voice filled with fear and love, "Jayvon, please, you gotta stop. I can't bear the thought of losing you. You mean more to me than anything, and I can't stand the idea of you risking your life in this, in this blood sport."

Jayvon found himself at a crossroads. The cheers of the crowd, the adrenaline of the fight—it was all he knew. But now, confronted with the fragility of his mortality, he hesitated. The doctor's words echoed in his mind, urging him to reconsider.

Chrissy, tears welling in her eyes, continued, "We can find another way, Jayvon. There are so many other things you're capable of. I believe in you, and I want a future with you. But you have to put your health first."

As the gravity of the situation pressed upon him, Jayvon felt the weight of Chrissy's words. The conflict within him was palpable—he was torn between the only life he knew and the love that beckoned him toward a safer future.

Reluctantly, Jayvon whispered, "I never thought I'd have to consider a life without fighting. But if it means a future with you, I'm done. I quit."

Jayvon thought he'd never utter that word for as long as he lived, but here he was saying it. The decision loomed heavily over his head. It was a daunting crossroads where the fight within himself had become the most challenging bout he had ever faced. But now it was over, just that fast.

She gave him a soft smile, then nodded toward the bathroom. "I'll be right back. Gotta freshen up."

Jayvon watched her walk away before stepping outside. The cool air hit his face as he pulled out a cigarette. He fumbled with his lighter, hands shaking slightly, still jittery from the fight and the doctor's news.

The repeated blows to your head have led to a condition known as Cavum septum pellucidum. It's a form of brain damage, and one more severe impact could prove fatal, or permanently blind you. I strongly advise you to reconsider your career in fighting, the doctor's voice echoed in his mind.

The words were a haunting reminder of his fragile state. He then heard the roars and cheers of the many crowds in his fights echoing in his ears. Then the feeling of his fists crashing against the warm flesh of his opponents. Their grunts. Their blood and sweat splattering against him. All the times the referee announced him as the winner.

I can't believe this shit is finally over, gang, Jayvon thought as he lit his cigarette, taking a long drag to calm his nerves. The nicotine buzzed through him, providing a temporary distraction from the grim prognosis. He expelled smoke from his nose and mouth and stared at the birds as they flew across the sky.

A sudden movement caught Jayvon's eye. He was surprised to see Purp and Stutter-Box walking in his direction, menacing expressions on their faces. Jayvon's brain screamed at him that he was in danger but he didn't heed the warning. His heart skipped a beat, and the cigarette fell from his lips. Instinctively, his hand went for his waistband, but then he recalled he'd left his gun in his whip. Panic surged through him as Purp reached inside his coat.

"Shit," Jayvon said under his breath, mind racing. He took a step back, preparing to make a run for it, but unfortunately, it was already too late.

Purp's hand emerged from his coat, holding a gold invitation. Jayvon's eyes bulged in surprise, and he let out a sigh of relief.

Purp chuckled, holding the invitation out to Jayvon. "Relax, my G. If me and my nigga Stutter were lookin' to air you out, we wouldn't have come straight up. Ain't that right, Stutter?"

"Y—Yep. An—and I would ha—have done th—the honors." Stutter-Box smirked wickedly, sizing Jayvon up.

Jayvon took the invitation, his hands still shaking. He glanced at the ornate card, the gold lettering shimmering in the sunlight. "Fuck is this?"

"It's an invite," Purp explained, with a casual tone. "To a private event. Big names, high stakes. Thought you might be interested."

Jayvon nodded slowly, his mind still racing. "What kinda event are we talking about?" he asked, slipping the invitation into his back pocket.

"You—you want me—me to—to tell—tell 'em?" Stutter-Box asked Purp.

"Hell naw. We'd be in front of this muthafucka all damn day," Purp replied. He explained to Jayvon that Bartise was having a fighting tournament in Bali and the winner would receive $5,000,000. He told Jayvon that he and anyone else he brought along could enter free of charge, but everyone else was breaking bread to get in. The only thing Jayvon had to worry about was the plane tickets to get to Bali.

"So you plan on comin'?" Purp inquired.

Jayvon picked up his cigarette and blew off the dirt it collected on the ground. "It's something for me to think about," he re-lit his cigarette and took another drag.

Purp grinned and patted Jayvon on the shoulder. "My man. Let's roll, Stutter."

Purp and Stutter Box turned and walked away, leaving Jayvon smoking his cigarette and contemplating his next move. The gold invitation offered a solution to his money problems. If he entered the tournament and won, he would have enough dough to finish paying off Draco, and replenish his stash.

Jayvon finished his cigarette and flicked away the butt. Chrissy emerged from the hospital, adjusting the strap of her purse on her shoulder and searching for him. She smiled when she saw him, and Jayvon felt a wave of warmth wash over him. Running over to him, she jumped into his arms, throwing her arms around his neck and wrapping her legs around his waist. She kissed him and laid her head against the side of his. He smiled as he pulled out his car keys and carried her over to his ride.

"You know it doesn't make any sense how much I love your ass," she said with her eyes closed.

"You ain't never lied, you should have your big ass head examined. That's for sure." Jayvon told her.

Chrissy snickered and smiled. "Shut up."

Jayvon nodded, glancing back at the spot where Purp and Stutter Box had stood. "Yeah, let's get out of here."

As they walked to the car, Jayvon couldn't shake the feeling that his world was about to change once again. The fight, the doctor's warning, and now the invitation—it all felt like pieces of a puzzle he hadn't figured out. But with Chrissy by his side, he felt ready to face whatever came next. Together, they could handle anything.

CHAPTER SEVEN

Jayvon, Chrissy, and Chyna sat around the dining room table, the low hum of three money-counting machines filling the tense silence. The machines whirred and clacked, processing piles of cash the gang had collected. The scent of stale cigar smoke lingered in the air, mingling with the faint aroma of money.

As the last bills were counted, Chrissy picked up a calculator and began crunching numbers. Her face fell as she saw the final amount, her frustration etched into her features. She sighed heavily and leaned back in her chair, staring at the ceiling. The ceiling fan turned lazily above, doing little to dispel the oppressive heat.

Jayvon noticed Chrissy's change in demeanor and asked, "What's the matter, Doll?"

Chrissy passed him the calculator without a word. Jayvon took it, glanced at the numbers, and his face mirrored her disappointment. He ran a hand down his face and massaged his chin, visibly agitated. His eyes, usually sharp and calculating, now looked tired and worn. Chyna, Augustus, and Bag Man watched the exchange with growing curiosity. Chyna's drummed his fingers rhythmically on the table, while Augustus puffed on a cigar, the end glowing bright red. Bag Man leaned against the wall, his arms folded across his chest.

"How we looking, bitch?" Bag Man asked, voice dripping concern.

Jayvon showed them the calculator. The collective mood in the room plummeted. Augustus took the cigar from his mouth, Chyna frowned, and Bag Man shook his head, all sharing the same look of disappointment.

Jayvon, hands on his hips, began pacing the floor, his frustration mounting. Suddenly, he snapped. "Fuuuuck!" he shouted, kicking over one of the dining room table chairs. The chair clattered to the ground, loud and jarring in the quiet space. The room fell eerily quiet after his outburst, the tension thick in the air. Chrissy, Chyna, Augustus, and Bag Man watched him with bated breath, waiting for his next move.

Jayvon stopped pacing and faced the group. "A'ight. Fuck it. Look, we're gonna see Draco's people tonight. They're expecting the entire five mill, but we'll request more time to get the rest. Hopefully, they'll give us the time we need."

Bag Man stepped forward, placing a reassuring hand on Jayvon's shoulder. "I think they will. We got nearly two mill in like a week. That's impressive."

"I agree," Augustus said, lighting the cigar that Chyna held out for him. The flame from the lighter briefly illuminated his features. "Once the spics see what we were able to accomplish in such a short time, their head honcho Draco definitely grant us a lil' more time to get the rest."

Chyna nodded, his expression earnest. "I think so too, big bruh."

"Me too, babe," Chrissy added, her voice soft but confident.

Jayvon looked around at the faces of his crew, seeing the confidence reflected in their eyes. He took a deep breath and nodded. "A'ight, let's get this bread loaded in these bags so we can make this drop." He began stuffing money into one of the duffle bags on the dining room table. The duffle bags were old and worn, the leather cracked from years of use. Chyna, Chrissy, and Bag Man quickly joined in, their movements swift. Augustus excused himself from the table to retrieve the guns they'd need for their mission. The sound of the safe opening in the adjacent room was faint but distinct.

As the group worked in silence, the weight of their situation hung over them. They knew the stakes were high but knew they had no choice but to press on. Jayvon glanced at each of them, silently grateful for their unwavering support of his cause.

"We're gonna make it through this, we have to," he said, his voice unwavering. "Pop is depending on us." he looked at the huge portrait of him, Chyna, and their father Trick. Trick held Chyna's legs as he sat on the back of his neck, holding their little league baseball trophy. Jayvon, smiling, stood beside his father holding up his baseball helmet and baseball bat triumphantly.

The rest of the gang nodded in agreement. They finished loading the duffle bags and prepared for the night ahead.

***

Bag Man and Chrissy stayed behind at the mansion while Angustus drove Jayvon and Chyna to Spanish Harlem. They double-parked outside of the brownstone where they were supposed to meet Shorty. The fellas double-checked their guns and walked up the steps. Jayvon knocked on the door while Chyna and Augustus watched their surroundings. The area they were in was spooky and eerily quiet. There weren't many people out in the streets that night but the few that were looked suspicious. They couldn't shake the feeling that a couple of knuckleheads were going to appear out of the shadows and make an attempt to rob them of the 1.5 million they busted their asses to collect.

A Black Puerto Rican dude draped in a poncho and toting an Uzi opened the front door and waved Jayvon and them inside. Once they'd cleared the threshold, the Black Puerto Rican dude stuck his head outside the door and looked around for anyone else in Jayvon's entourage. Locking the door behind him, he turned to a couple of Puerto Ricans pinning Jayvon and them against the wall. One of them held them at gunpoint while the other patted them down thoroughly. He dropped the guns he found during the search inside the duffle bag Jayvon brought and picked it up.

Jayvon, Chyna, and Augustus were escorted down the long corridor, which opened to a small living room, and a slightly bigger kitchen. Shorty was sitting at the kitchen table with two money counters. There was also an ashtray with half of a blunt burning in it and a .357 magnum revolver lying next to it. The Puerto Rican man who relieved Jayvon of the duffle bag dropped it on the table in front of Shorty. The little Puerto Rican man didn't waste any time unzipping the bag and looking at all the cash. He whistled thinking about all the things money like that could buy. He grabbed one of the stacks out of the duffle bag and ran his finger over its top. He tossed the stack back inside the bag and looked at it again.

"So this is what five million dollars looks like, huh? I can't lie. I was expecting a couple more bags than this." Shorty said to no one in particular. Right then, Jayvon, Chyna, and Augustus exchanged glances, knowing the money in the duffle bag wasn't the full amount Draco demanded from them.

Jayvon cleared his throat and spoke up. "Look, bro, we couldn't get together five million dollars in such a short time. That's 1.5 right there in front of you. I'm thinking, maybe your boss will give us a lil' more time to get the rest of the dough together."

Shorty laid back in his chair and blew a frustrating breath at the ceiling. He picked up his burnout cellphone, scrolled through his contacts until he found the name and number he was looking for, and pressed the *call* button. The phone rang at least six times before Draco finally picked up. Jayvon knew it was him. He had one of those voices that stood out among others.

Shorty's conversation with Draco was shorter than a mosquito's dick. They swapped a few words in Spanish. Then the next thing Jayvon knew, Shorty had disconnected the call and tossed his cellular upon the table.

Shorty, keeping his eyes pinned on Jayvon, leaned back and drummed his fingers on the tabletop. Jayvon became nervous. He could feel the sweat sliding down the side of his face. On top of that his heart was beating so fast, he thought it would leap out of his chest. He glanced at Chyna and Augustus. He could tell they were nervous too, but they were doing a much better job at hiding it than him.

Niggaz took our guns so now we're butt-ass naked with our dicks in our hands. I don't know what's gon' be these dudes play, but I'm not finna just lie my neck on the choppin' block for 'em to chop my head off, Jayvon thought. He zeroed in on the revolver lying on the table. If Chyna and Augustus followed his lead and engaged the armed Puerto Ricans, he may be able to get his hands on Shorty's revolver and turn the tables on them. It was a long shot, but it was worth the risk.

"Jefe is willing to grant you a courtesy one-month extension to get the rest of the money," Shorty delivered the news. The news lifted a weight off of Jayvon's shoulders. He sighed with relief on the inside.

"In one month you'll get the rest of the bag. That's my word." Jayvon swore. Although he didn't know how the hell he was going to get his hands on that kind of bread in a month, he was going to do everything in his power to get it.

"Good," Shorty replied, removing their guns from the duffle bag and placing them on the tabletop. "I believe these belong to you." He saw the hesitation in Jayvon and them to get their pistols. "It's okay. Go ahead." he swept his hand over the cache of weapons.

Jayvon, Chyna, and Augustus picked up their guns and tucked them inside their waistbands. The Black Puerto Rican threw his head toward the hallway and escorted them to the front door.

***

In the confines of the county jail, nestled within its concrete walls and barbed wire, lived Draco and his notorious henchmen. Once feared on the streets, they now ruled their kingdom within their cells.

It all began with a daring scheme—a ransom demand of $5 million to ensure the safety of Jayvon and Chyna's father Trick. The plan went off without a hitch, and soon Draco and his crew found themselves with a hefty portion of the ransom money in their possession.

Within the facility's walls, Draco and his henchmen lived like kings. While regular inmates scraped by on meager rations and basic amenities, Draco's crew enjoyed luxuries unimaginable to others behind bars.

Their first order of business was securing the best accommodations money could buy. They bribed guards and prison officials to ensure they were housed in the most comfortable cells, complete with plush mattresses, personal televisions, and even mini-fridges stocked with contraband snacks and drinks. But their lavish lifestyle didn't stop there. Draco and his henchmen could procure a myriad of forbidden goods and services within the prison walls. From gourmet meals prepared by fellow inmates who owed them favors to illicit drugs smuggled in by corrupt guards, his crew wanted nothing.

Their influence extended beyond material comforts. With their newfound wealth and power, Draco and his crew established a network of loyal followers within the jail, earning respect and deference from inmates and staff.

While other inmates toiled away in the prison's workshops and facilities, Draco and his henchmen spent days lounging in their grandiose cells, orchestrating their criminal empire from behind bars. They were untouchable, their reign within the prison walls unchallenged.

But even as they lived in luxury, there was always the looming threat of justice catching up to them. Every day was a delicate balancing act for Draco and his henchmen, navigating the treacherous waters of jail life while clinging to the spoils of their ill-gotten gains.

Yet, for now, they basked in their newfound status as jail royalty, enjoying a life of excess and indulgence that few could dream of behind bars.

Draco and his henchmen gathered around a makeshift table adorned with stolen silverware and fine linens smuggled in from the outside world. The aroma of a gourmet meal, prepared by their trusted kitchen accomplice, wafted through the air, mingling with the sound of laughter and clinking glasses.

"Tonight, we feast like kings!" Draco declared, raising his glass high. "To us, and the spoils of our conquest!"

The henchmen cheered in unison, their voices echoing off the cold, unforgiving walls of their concrete fortress. As they settled into their seats, the conversation turned to reminiscing about their past exploits and planning for the future. Draco regaled his comrades with tales of their daring heists and narrow escapes, each story punctuated by roars of laughter and nods of admiration. But amidst the revelry, there was a moment of reflection as one of the henchmen stood to propose a toast to their leader.

"To Draco, the man who took us under his wing when nobody else would," he began, his voice thick with emotion. "For always looking out for us, for taking care of our families when we couldn't. Here's to you, boss." The henchmen raised their glasses again, their eyes shining with gratitude and respect for the man who had become their leader in this unforgiving world. Draco's chest swelled with pride as he looked around at his loyal companions, his heart warmed by their loyalty. In that moment, surrounded by friends and allies, he felt invincible, as if nothing could tear them apart.

As they clinked their glasses together in a final toast, Draco knew that no matter what challenges lay ahead, they would face them together, united in their bond of brotherhood and loyalty. And as long as they had each other, they would always be kings, even in the darkest depths of their jail kingdom.

CHAPTER EIGHT

The city was a blur of lights and shadows as Chyna sped through the streets. D'Anthony closed his eyes and stuck his head out of the passenger window, letting the wind blow against his face. Chyna grinned as he glanced at his homeboy, thinking of how much he reminded him of a dog with his head hanging out of the window.

D'Anthony settled back into the passenger seat, letting the window up and taking the roach end of a blunt from the ashtray. He set fire to the tip and blew out a cloud. "I'm telling you, big homie, as good as the kid is feeling, we can collect on that five mill tonight."

"Yeah. That weed got cho ass far gone," Chyna grinned. "We can getta chunk of that dough, but not the whole thang in one night."

"We could if we knew some cartel niggaz to hit."

"You're talking crazy now, lil' bruh. I'd go up against anyone with my gun, but the cartel, I'm not tryna see if I don't have to."

As soon as Chyna drove up to a red traffic light, a van screeched as it came to a diagonal stop in front of him. He and Chyna went to draw heat, but masked niggaz AK-47s beat them to it. Their assault rifles had one hundred drums. The masked niggaz pushed the van's door open further and one of them started barking orders.

"Anyone of you dudes move, I'll blow you outta yo Nikes. Comprende?" The skinnest masked man asked. Chyna and D'Anthony nodded. "Okay. You behind the wheel, slowly open the door, and get outta the car. You try any slick shit and that's yo ass, my guy.'"

Chyna followed the skinny masked nigga's orders and laid the side of his face on the ground. D'Anthony followed behind him, doing what the masked gunman asked of him. With a sway of his AK-47, the skinny masked nigga motioned his partner over to Chyna and D'Anthony. After he restrained their wrists behind their back, he gagged their mouths and pulled a black pillowcase over their heads. Together, the masked gunmen roughly pulled the boys up and ushered them to their van. Inside the van, one of the masked gunmen held Chyna and D'Anthony at gunpoint, ordering them to lie on their stomachs. The other one duct-taped their wrists, and mouths, and threw a black sack over their heads.

***

Thirty minutes later, the masked niggaz that hopped out on Chyna and D'Anthony, walked them through the side door of a warehouse at gunpoint. The boys' senses were overwhelmed with barking, sweat, urine, and dog shit. They conceded to the order to stop that one of their kidnappers gave, and then the black sacks were snatched off their heads. They narrowed their eyes and turned their faces from the LED worklights until the soft burn lifted from their eyes. When they turned back around they saw Dolph with his bare, hairy chest exposed, dressed in gray slacks and leather dress shoes. He was sweating like he'd been picking cotton in the scorching Mississippi sun. A chain leash was wrapped around his fist, and he was having a tough time keeping his barking Rottweiler from chewing up Chyna and D'Anthony's asses.

Five men wearing black sacks over their heads with their wrists tied behind their backs sat on their knees before Dolph. Chyna and D'Anthony's mind wondered about the possibilities that could have landed the men in their predicament. Although they weren't sure what they'd done, they knew they had to have wronged Dolph on some level since they were at his mercy.

"Just the lil' niggaz I've been dyin' to see," Dolph smiled wickedly, displaying his wonderfully white teeth.

The Rottweiler was barking even louder now, slobbering everywhere. "Roof, roof, roof, roof, roof!"

"Shut the fuck up!" Dolph angrily punched and kicked the hound. It yelped but did as it was told. "Y'all niggaz cut them boys loose so they can remove that tape from their mouths."

Once Chyna and D'Anthony were free of their restraints, they peeled the duct-tape from their mouths and looked at Dolph.

"Yo, Dolph, what's this about?" Chyna asked.

"I mean, it must be pretty serious for you to have niggaz jump outta van and snatch ya mans up," D'Anthony added.

Dolph took his time latching his Rottweiler's leash to a nearby pillar before turning around to address his little homies. "Oh, best believe it is," he took a gun from the small of his back and cocked it, chambering a round in its head. The sight of the pole made Chyna and D'Anthony uneasy. They were expecting Dolph to blast them. "You see, there's a crew within my crew that's been juxin' shit in my city and not kicking up a cut to the Gods. You know, the three wise men. My big brother King Morpheus, and his left and right hand, King Shyne and King Yak." He allowed what he said to sink into Chyna and D'Anthony's brains as he walked around the five men on their knees before him. He stopped behind the last man in the row. "I have it on good authority to believe these five were the ones that went rogue, so I must see to it that every one of these assholes getta bullet to the back of their skulls. Unless you two are harboring some info that'll lead me to the real bandits hittin' licks in my town," he looked at D'Anthony and then Chyna. They thought he knew about them making scratch, and not breaking bread with the powers that be, but they weren't sure. So they decided to keep their mouths shut and see how things played out.

D'Anthony swallowed the spit in his mouth and shook his head. "Nah. I haven't heard anything about anyone else making moves out here," he assured Dolph. "So if you got it on good authority these niggaz been doing their own thang, handle yo' candle, big homie."

Dolph's eyes shifted to Chyna. "How about you, Chyna? You catch wind of something out there?" Chyna hesitantly shook his head, and Dolph pointed his piece at the back of his intended victim's skull. As he applied pressure to the trigger, Chyna's abrupt hollering froze him cold.

"Stop!" Chyna's voice echoed throughout the warehouse.

Dolph looked back at him with a raised eyebrow. "Something you wanna get off ya chest, young king?"

"It was me," Chyna said, dropping his head. He looked back up at Dolph, prepared to face his punishment. "I was the one takin' gigs for profit and not shooting you big bruh and them their tribute."

Dolph lowered his gun, giving Chyna his undivided attention. "So, it was you by yo' self? You went on missions solo?"

D'Anthony glanced at the ground and said, "Fuck," under his breath. He looked back up at Dolph, fearlessly. "Nah. I was with 'em. We did those jobs together."

Dolph had a look of disappointment on his face as he walked toward Chyna, tucking his stick at the small of his back. He placed his hands on his shoulders and looked into his eyes. "I'm proud of you, lil' bro, you manned up and dropped the truth, raw and uncut." he ruffled his head. "Normally, I'd drop a nigga right where he stood for what chu did, but I got mad love for you. I can't let chu slide though...'cause if I did every King in our organization would be tryna ice skate, nah mean?"

Chyna nodded. "Look, Dolph, I know what I did was wrong, but it was for a good reason, gang. You see—"

Dolph placed his finger on Chyna's lips and shushed him. "Shhhhh. It doesn't even matter, my G. You've gotta face the music now." he hugged him, took a breath, and kissed him on the cheek. "I love you, young king."

"I love you too, Dolph," Chyna replied nervously.

Dolph gave a slight nod to the Kings that brought Chyna and D'Anthony to the warehouse. They slipped the straps of their assault rifles over their shoulders and drew knives from the sheath on their hip. They busied themselves removing the black sacks from the five men that were on their knees and cutting the ropes restraining their wrists. Abruptly, Dolph kneed Chyna in his balls and kicked him in the side of the head. As he fell toward the ground, Dolph attacked D'Anthony next. Before the kid could mount a decent defense, Dolph gave him a shot to his liver, dropping him to his knee. When D'Anthony looked up, Dolph was launching his leg toward his face. He held up his hand to block the assault, but Dolph's leg was stronger than he thought. The boy caught the full impact of his sneaker in the head and spilled onto the pavement.

Dolph signaled the five men to beat the brakes off Chyna and D'Anthony. He watched as fists and sneakers came down hard and fast on them. The boys tried to fight back, but Dolph's assault had left them too weak and vulnerable to defend themselves. Once Dolph felt they had enough, he called for the punishment to cease, throwing up his hand. The five men stopped on cue, walking away. Chyna and D'Anthony, both bleeding and dirty, lay unconscious on the ground.

Dolph nodded in satisfaction as he looked at the handiwork of his men. He swopped a few words with the Kings that brought

Chyna and D'Anthony to the warehouse, retrieved his Rottweiler, and walked out of the building whistling Dixie.

***

Chyna stirred awake in the warehouse, wincing from the beating he and D'Anthony got from the Kings. He spat blood on the ground and jabbed a loose tooth with his tongue. When he looked at D'Anthony, he was just coming to with a rat snooping about on his chest. As soon as he noticed the filthy rodent he smacked it off him and slowly got up on his feet, grimacing. He extended his hand to Chyna and pulled him on his feet.

"You a'ight, gang?" Chyna asked D'Anthony.

"Nah. I'm real fucked up, yo, them niggaz beat our asses like we stole something." D'Anthony frowned, rubbing his aching side. "The trip is, what we stole, wasn't even their shit."

Chyna laughed and threw his arm around D'Anthony's shoulders. "What're we gonna do, lil' bruh? This is what we signed up for. Smell me?"

Chyna walked out of the warehouse with D'Anthony under his arm. They were surprised when they saw his whip parked inside the parking lot of the warehouse. It was like it had been sitting there waiting for them to come out the entire time. Chyna figured Dolph must have had a couple of the Kings double back and get it. This meant there wasn't any love loss to the situation and the big homie still considered them good in his book.

Chyna patted his jeans pockets and came up with his cellphone and car keys. When the Kings snatched him and D'Anthony, he clearly remembered them taking both items. So, they must have planted them back on him while he was knocked out cold. Chyna tapped D'Anthony and they made their way over to his vehicle. He started it up and drove out to Red Hook projects.

CHAPTER NINE

Once Chyna pulled up outside D'Anthony's side of the projects, he shifted his car into park and allowed its engine to run.

"Yo, gang, I'ma get up witchu tomorrow, a'ight?" Chyna told D'Anthony.

Anthony, who was busy studying his bruises and cuts in the sun visor mirror, nodded and shook up with Chyna.

"A'ight then," D'Anthony replied, "Hit me up, and lemme know you made it in the house."

"No doubt, love fool."

"Love."

Chyna watched as D'Anthony hopped out of his car and jogged inside the projects. Once he saw the young nigga enter his building, he cranked up his ride and drove away.

Chyna fished through the graveyard of blunt roaches in his ashtray until he found one of reasonable size. He didn't have a lighter, so he used the one that came installed in his whip. The tip of his bleezy glowed with an ember. He sucked on the end of it and blew out a cloud of smoke. He thought about going home to shower and nurse his wounds but reasoned it was best to slide out to his brother's crib. There was no use of him avoiding Jayvon because he would eventually see his wounds from his beating anyway so he thought it was best to get it over with now. At least that was his thoughts on the matter now.

Chyna was sure that Jayvon was going to flip out once he saw the Kings' work. If he knew his brother, he would be ready to give all parties involved with putting hands on his little brother the business. It wouldn't matter to him what the reason behind it was. Big brother would want blood to answer with blood. Chyna couldn't blame him either, because if someone had hurt his brother, he'd be looking to give their asses that work too.

Chyna wasn't sweating what Dolph had the Kings do to him because he knew he had it coming. He'd broken the rules so he should have been ostracized, or killed. He knew that Dolph and Bocka fucked with him from the heart and that was the only reason why mercy was shown and he was giving a pass. Chyna knew without a doubt that should some other unlucky bastard have winded up on the wrong end of Dolph's wrath, he'd be somewhere buried and rotting in an unmarked grave.

With his brother on his mind, Chyna attached his cellular to the holder on the dashboard and powered it on. He had thirty missed calls and most of them were from Jayvon and them.

Chyna managed to smile through his busted lips. He couldn't front even if he wanted to. It felt good having people in his life who gave a fucka 'bout his well-being.

"Siri, call big bruh."

Siri replied instantly, "Calling Big Bruh."

Christy answered Jayvon's jack on the third ring.

"What up sis?"

"Chyna, where in the hell are you? Boy, everyone has been worried sick."

"I'm around, sis. Y'all at the house?"

"Yeah. Augustus and Bag Man just came back from looking for you."

"Aww, y'all really do love a nigga," Chyna grinned.

"Bro, stop playing where are you?"

"On my way there, tell bruh and them I'm 'bouta pull up."

"Kay. Love you."

"Love you more. One."

Chyna disconnected the call and stole a look at his appearance through the sun visor mirror. Not only was he swollen and lumped up, he had blood clots in his eye, and dry blood in his nostrils.

"Mannn, this nigga Jayvon 'bouta wig out." Chyna closed the sun visor and focused his attention back on the streets.

***

Jayvon and Chrissy were talking when Chyna walked through the front door. They were shocked to see him bloody and bruised. Chrissy sprang to her feet and dashed over to him, examining his injuries.

"What the hell happened to you?" Chrissy asked, her voice filled with concern.

"Dolph found out about D'Anthony and me juxin' and not giving the Kings of Thieves their share of the profits," Chyna winced, as Chrissy gently touched one of many of his swollen bruises. "He had some of the guys kick our ass."

"Punk muthafucka," Jayvon roared, punching a hole through the wall in a fit of rage. His outburst brought Augustus and Bag Man running into the living room, pool sticks in hand. They had been playing pool in the game room when they heard the loud noise.

"What's going on?" Augustus demanded, eyes wide.

Jayvon recounted what Chyna had told them, his anger palpable. He grabbed a small remote from the coffee table, pointed it at a wall of family portraits, and pressed a button. The wall did a 180-degree turn, revealing an arsenal. "We're hittin' the Kings of Thieves tonight, for what they did to bro."

"Nigga think because he's gotta goddamn army behind 'em he can just handle my people however he wants? Gang got me fucked up. Here," Jayvon tossed Chyna a Glock 50 after loading it. He then started passing out white Kevlar bulletproof vests.

Chyna tried to reason with him again. "Bro, we got beat down 'cause we weren't giving them their cut. Maybe we sh—"

Jayvon cut him off, his forehead wrinkled with animosity. "Granny and Pop Pop would turn over in their grave if they knew I let niggaz put their paws on you and I didn't run rec on 'em. Come on, Mighty Mouse," Jayvon called Chyna by his nickname as he walked by him, nudging his arm. Chyna looked down at the Glock in his hand, then at Jayvon as he walked toward the front door. He was torn between loyalty and reason, unsure of what to do. Seeing his hesitation, Chrissy ran to the front door and blocked their path.

"You can't murder Dolph and risk being killed or imprisoned. Your father is counting on you to deliver the rest of the five million dollars to Draco's boys."

"Only niggaz getting killed are the ones wearing purple and gold, lil' baby," Jayvon retorted. "So you don't have jack to worry about. Now, move yo' lil' ass out the—"

"I'm pregnant," Chrissy blurted, catching everyone by surprise. Silence fell over the mansion until Jayvon spoke up, holding the side of Chrissy's face and looking into her eyes.

"You serious, Doll? No cap?" Jayvon asked, his voice softer.

Chrissy nodded, tears filling up in her eyes. "I found out three days ago. I would have told you sooner, but—"

Jayvon interrupted her with a kiss. He hugged her tightly, and she wrapped her arms around his neck, tears sliding down her cheeks. "I love you, Von. I don't wanna chance something happening to you and our child growing up without its father."

"Nothing is gonna happen to me, I swear on everythang," Jayvon assured her. "You got my seed growin' inside of you so I gotta be here to make sure y'all straight."

Smiling, Jayvon turned around to the fellas. "Guess what, gang, y'all gonna be uncles," he announced, voice dripping joy.

The room erupted in cheers and applause. Chyna, Augustus, and Bag Man clapped Jayvon on the back, their congratulations mingling with laughter. They turned to Chrissy, each giving her a loving hug and a kiss on the cheek.

"That's what's up, yo! Congrats to both of y'all," Chyna exclaimed, his grin widening.

"Thank you, family," Chrissy said, beaming. "I want y'all to be the godfathers of our child. I wanna do it right, with a ceremony in church and everything."

The men exchanged glances, nodding in agreement. "We'd be honored," Augustus said sincerely.

Just then, Bag Man cleared his throat, his face turning serious. "I know we're all excited about having a new niece or nephew, and I hate to be the nigga to bring this up, but I have to," he said, holding his M-16 assault rifle. "Are we letting Dolph slide after what he did to shorty, or are we still getting active with 'em?" His eyes scanned Jayvon, Augustus, and Chyna, waiting for their response.

A tense silence settled over the room. Chrissy looked at Jayvon, worry reflected in her eyes. Though she didn't speak, her gaze was a silent plea."

Jayvon met her eyes, feeling the weight of her unspoken request. He took a deep breath, then turned back to his crew. "Dolph can keep his life for now," he said reluctantly. "But only until I figure out a way to take him down without putting myself in harm's way. We need to be smart about this."

Chyna, Augustus, and Bag Man exchanged looks of understanding. Bag Man nodded, gripping his rifle tighter. "A'ight, bitch. We'll play it your way."

Jayvon nodded, feeling a bit of the tension ease in his shoulders. He reached for Chrissy's hand, giving it a reassuring squeeze. "We'll get through this," he promised her. "Together."

Chrissy smiled, her eyes filled with gratitude. "I know we will," she whispered, leaning into him.

The gang stood together, ready to face whatever challenges lay ahead.

***

After everyone's excitement about the baby calmed down, the gang started thinking of ways to get the bread they needed to pay off Draco. Although the boys had several get-money schemes they could execute to get the amount they needed, busting all those moves would exceed the time frame they were given. So when Chrissy announced she had a way to get the loot they needed and then some they were all ears.

Chrissy stood poised before Jayvon, Bag Man, Augustus, and Chyna, her eyes reflecting a hint of nervous anticipation. "There's this major drug lord type nigga," she began, her voice steady yet urgent. "A friend and I used to provide the entertainment for at private parties, back when I was shakin' ass at Big Daddy's. Anyway, when dude would get drunk and shovel that powder up his nose, he'd start bragging about how many kilos he moved in a week and how much bread he had."

Jayvon leaned forward, his brows furrowing with curiosity. "How much are we talkin'?" he asked, voice low and intent.

Chrissy paused for effect, then dropped the bombshell. "$150 million," she declared, watching their reactions closely. There wasn't a soul in the living room that wasn't amazed by the dollar amount she'd thrown out.

Augustus let out a low whistle, shaking his head in disbelief. "Sheesh. That's a damn fortune," he said.

"And here's the kicker," Chrissy continued, her tone conspiratorial. "I bet if we can get his ass saucy again, he'll spill everything when wanna know about that loot—where it's hidden, how to access it."

Chyna nodded thoughtfully, rubbing his chin. "We need just over $3 million to save pops from Draco," he reminded them, voice firm. "This could be our only shot at hitting that kinda payday."

Jayvon considered the implications, weighing the risks against the potential reward. After a moment of contemplation, he looked at Chrissy nodding. "A'ight," he said firmly. "Let's do it. Call 'em."

Chrissy grabbed her cellphone, her fingers moving swiftly, searching through her list of contacts for Finesse's number. Once she found it, she tapped it. A man with a hint of a Dominicano accent answered, and she adopted a sultry tone. "Hey there, handsome, it's Chris," she purred, a slight smile playing on her lips. "Remember me?"

Finesse's voice on the other end was smooth, tinged with curiosity. "Shiiiit, how can I forget sucha beautiful woman, especially with all the good times we've had? What's on your mind, mami?"

Chrissy glanced briefly at Jayvon, who nodded subtly. "Well, I've been reminiscing about our wild times," she continued smoothly, her voice laced with suggestion. "How about we catch up tomorrow night? I'm looking forward to suckin' on that big Spanish dick and having you blow my back out."

"Mmmm," Finesse said, clearly turned on by her dirty talk. Though she couldn't see it, he had a handful of himself then. "Only if you promise to bring your friend witchu. What's her name? Six or Sex, something like that?"

Chrissy frowned as she tried thinking of who he was talking about. "You mean Jos—I mean, uh, Sex Pistol?"

"Yeah. That's her." Finesse replied. He was thinking of a time he was smashing Sex Pistol from the back while she ate Chrissy's pussy.

"She may be busy, but I'll see what I can do," Chrissy assured him. "You remember my quote?"

"I most certainly do," he said. "I'm sure you recall the address to my home. How about tomorrow night around say, uh, 9 o'clock?"

"Sounds like a plan, papi."

"Should I send one my car?"

"Nah. We'll just take my girl's car." Chrissy glanced back at the others, a spark of excitement in her eyes. "Be sure you have that favorite champagne of yours.'Cause this is gonna be a night to remember."

"You got it, baby."

"Muah."

Chrissy kissed him through the phone and disconnected the call. She smiled, jumping around and clapping her hands. She stopped when she looked at the boys and they weren't as excited as she was. There was a tense silence hanging in the air. Jayvon, Chyna, Augustus, and Bag Man had acknowledged the risk ahead. Chrissy picked up what was on their mind like a psychic. She knew they were dealing with some heavy shit, but they had to do what they had to do if they were going to keep Draco from killing Trick.

Chrissy glanced at her watch. "Look, Joe is still at the club. I'ma drop by there and see if she wants in on this opportunity," she grabbed her purse and kissed everyone on their cheek goodbye.

Once Chrissy was gone, the boys began preparing for the heist, each one focused and ready for the dangerous challenge that lay ahead.

CHAPTER TEN

In the smoky, dim-lit confines of Big Daddy's, the air hummed with anticipation as the rhythmic pulse of music reverberated through the establishment. Amidst the swirling haze of colorful lights, a lone figure moved with hypnotic grace upon the stage, her body was a symphony of curves and shadows.

She was an exotic dancer, a siren of the night whose every move seemed to command the attention of every eye in the establishment. With each twist and turn of her nimble form, she wove a spell of desire and fantasy, drawing her audience into a world of pure escapism.

Chrissy sat in the back of the club, camouflaged by the shadows, nursing a glass of cranberry juice. The music was so loud inside of Big Daddy's she could barely hear herself think. It wasn't like she needed to though. At least not now she didn't. Her eyes were locked on the half-naked young lady dancing provocatively on stage. The name on her driver's license read Josephine Milhouse, but she did her thing under Sex Pistol. Josephine was a petite, dark caramel-complexion shorty with fake boobs and just enough ass for a trick to grab two hands full. She was cute in the face, with exaggerated long hair that flowed down her back and over her star-studded areolas. She didn't look a day over fourteen, but she'd just made it to the legal drinking age.

Little mama had been running the streets for as long as she could remember, getting money both ways, legally and illegally, which was why she could afford to take care of her five kids, her crib, push a beemer truck, and take trips whenever she liked.

Josephine wore a brown cowboy hat, blue jean denim chaps, and brown leather boots, with spurs. Holding out her long tongue, and keeping her eyes on Chrissy, she gyrated her hips and spun her ivory-handled, nickel-plated revolvers in her hands. She spun around, did the splits to the floor, and came back up, firing the blank rounds from her colts.

Her audience hollered, whistled, and threw dollars at her. The money landed on the stage, but she didn't pay it any mind. She continued to spin her twin pistols, moving her body to the loud music, while the lights danced around her.

As the final notes of the music faded into silence, Josephine gracefully descended from the stage, her skin glistening with sweat beneath the sultry glow of the lights. The crowd's applause washed over her like a warm embrace, a tangible testament to the power of her performance.

With an arrogant smile, Josephine made her way through a throng of patrons, collecting the generous tips thrown at her during her performance. The crisp sound of bills being counted filled the air, a symphony of currency that spoke volumes of her success.

But amidst the chaos of the gentlemen's club, there was a moment of quiet introspection as Josephine slipped into the relative privacy of the locker room. Here, away from the prying eyes of horny men, she shed the persona of Sex Pistol, The Exotic Temptress, and revealed the woman beneath.

With practiced efficiency, Josephine peeled away the layers of her costume, each article of clothing was a testament to the artistry of her craft. The soft rustle of fabric filled the air as she slipped into modest attire.

As she gathered her belongings and prepared to leave, a sense of satisfaction washed over her like a wave crashing into a shore. In that moment of solitude, she knew she'd done more than entertain; she'd transported her audience to a world where the boundaries of reality faded away, if only for a fleeting moment.

Josephine slammed her locker's door and was surprised to see Chrissy leaning against the one beside it. Before she could utter a word, her former coworker beat her to the punch.

"You tryna make some money?"

***

Jayvon, Chyna, and Augustus stood around his bed, meticulously cleaning assault rifles and loading ammo into clips. The room was filled with the metallic clicks and clacks of weapons being prepared, in contrast to the tense silence in the bedroom. The air was thick with the smell of gun oil, a shared understanding that tonight was pivotal.

Bag Man walked into the bedroom, his presence commanding attention. Draped over his arm was an expensive knockoff designer suit encased in a plastic covering, and in his other hand, he carried a sleek silver briefcase.

"Here you go," Bag Man said, voice low and steady. He passed the suit to Jayvon. "Try it on."

Jayvon held up the suit, inspecting the fine details and craftsmanship. "Looks legit," he muttered, setting it aside. He turned his attention to the briefcase. With a quick, practiced motion, he popped the locks and opened them to reveal lifelike replicas of Finesse's face and hands.

Chyna and Augustus stopped what they were doing, their eyes widening in awe at the uncanny realism of the mask and gloves.

"Damn," Chyna said, laying his assault rifle on the bed. "That looks real as hell." He couldn't resist trying on the face mask. Moving to the mirror, he adjusted it carefully and stared at his reflection with fascination and disbelief. "Look at me," he laughed. "I'm Finesse!"

Augustus, meanwhile, slipped one of the glove hands onto his own, flexing his fingers and marveling at how natural it felt. "This is some next-level stuff," he said, turning his hand over to examine the details.

Jayvon took the mask and gloves from his friends. "Alright, let me give it a go," he said. He began to put them on, the silicone fitting snugly and molding to his features. He then slipped into the designer suit, the transformation almost complete. With the final adjustments, he stood before the mirror, his heart pounding with anticipation.

Augustus, Chyna, and Bag Man gathered behind him, their reflections creating a powerful image in the glass. Jayvon turned to face them, and they all nodded in unison. With the mask, gloves, and suit on, Jayvon was a spitting image of Finesse. The resemblance was eerie, down to the smallest detail.

Chyna whistled, impressed. "Man, if I didn't know better, I'd say you were him."

Augustus nodded in agreement. "Yeah, this is crazy. You look exactly like Finesse."

Bag Man stepped forward, his eyes scanning Jayvon from head to toe. "It's perfect," he said. "No one will be able to tell the difference. Just remember, stick to the plan. Don't get cocky."

Jayvon took a deep breath, steeling himself for the task ahead. "I gotchu," he replied. "Let's get this done."

His friends watched him, knowing that what lay ahead was fraught with danger. Yet, in that shared glance, there was also a silent understanding. They were ready.

***

Chrissy and Josephine walked briskly to Josephine's murky-blue E-class Mercedes Benz. The cool night air did little to calm their thudding hearts as they settled into the luxurious taupe leather seats. Josephine started the engine, the car came back to life as they drove away from the mansion, leaving the boys behind.

"I'm not gonna front, girl, I'ma lil' tense," Chrissy said, her voice shaky yet exhilarated. She pulled down the visor mirror and applied the sedative-laced lipstick Augustus had given her, her hands steady despite the adrenaline coursing through her veins.

"Tell me about it," Josephine replied, glancing at Chrissy as she navigated the dark streets. "But we're gon' pull this shit off, and get this money."

Chrissy nodded, clicking the lipstick tube shut and slipping it into her purse. "No doubt, sis."

Glancing at Chrissy, Josephine could see she was uptight. "Don't wet it, we got this." she smiled and outstretched her fist. Chrissy smiled back and touched fists with her. "Heyyy, that's my bitch."

Josephine cranked up the volume on "Realest Niggas" by 50 Cent and Notorious B.I.G. as she raced up the road, leaving debris behind.

***

The drive to the mansion felt like it took a century, but eventually, they arrived at their destination. The opulent estate loomed before them, its grandeur almost mocking their humble beginnings. No matter how many times the girls saw Finesse's crib, they never ceased to be fascinated by it. Their reaction was like kids seeing Christmas lights. They swore up and down that one day they would own mansions just as big as the kingpin's mansion.

Josephine parked her Mercedes in front of Finesse's place where two of his security guards stood watch. They stepped out, their heels clicking against the cobble-stone driveway as they walked up the steps. The security guards, holding MAC-10s, engaged the girls, their imposing figures casting long shadows. Chrissy and Josephine exchanged a nervous glance as the guards approached, their weapons glinting in the dim light.

"Long time no see, fellas," Chrissy smiled as she chewed her gum.

"Mmmm. True indeed. Long time no see." one of the guards replied, looking them up and down alongside the other. Their eyes lingered a moment too long on the girls' revealing attire.

"Whatcha got there?" one of the guards demanded, taking one of the bottles of champagne the girls held.

"Just some refreshments for the party," Josephine said sweetly, batting her eyelashes.

The guard inspected the bottle thoroughly, trying to find something suspicious. "Armand de Brignac Ace of Spades Brut Rose," he read what it said on the pretty rose-tinted glass bottle. "Pink champagne, huh?" he passed the champagne back to Josephine.

"Yeah. That's one of Finesse's favorites," Chrissy informed him. She was surprised when the other guard took her purse and rifled through it.

He came up with a small transparent Ziploc bag of pink cocaine. "Pink coke, huh? Looks like jefe plans on having one hell of a party tonight."

The other guard took the Ziploc bag of pink coke from his co-worker. "Say, uh, you girls don't mind if I take a little bump before you go inside, do ya?"

Chrissy snatched the bag of coke back and dropped it inside her purse. "No, my brother, you've gotta get your own," she mimicked the classic commercial.

Josephine leaned in close to the guard Chrissy snatched the bag of cocaine from, her lips brushing against his ear as she whispered a flirtatious remark. "You know, I thinka men in suits are very, very, very sexy." A faint blush crept into the guard's cheeks as he smiled.

"You think so?" he asked, licking his lips.

"Definitely," Josephine replied, her hand resting lightly on his arm. "Maybe after my girl and I wrap things up with your jefe, we can get to know each other better on a more intimate level, what do ya say?"

"I'd say, 'yes'." the guard replied, feeling Josephine's lips brush slightly against his.

Meanwhile, Chrissy charmed the other guard with her quick wit and playful banter. "You must work out a lot. Those muscles look rock hard," she said, running a finger down his arm. The guard couldn't help but chuckle, his tough exterior was melting away in the warmth of her charm.

"You like what you see, mama, huh?" the guard asked, flexing his bicep, its muscle looked like it would split the fabric of his sleeve.

"Oooooou, absolutely," Chrissy acted impressed, feeling his rock-hard bicep. "I think you deserve a lil' reward." She leaned in and kissed his lips, leaving a perfect imprint of her lipstick.

Josephine, not to be outdone, leaned in and kissed her guard, leaving her mark on his lips. "Something to remember me by," she whispered with a wink.

The guards, now thoroughly charmed, allowed the girls access to their boss's mansion.

"Alright, you're clear," the first guard said, a smile tugging at the corner of his mouth.

With a final wink and a saucy smile, Chrissy and Josephine sashayed past the guards and into the mansion, their hearts pounding with exhilaration. As they disappeared into the depths of the lavish estate, the guards watched them go, adjusting their hard-ons in their slacks.

CHAPTER ELEVEN

Inside the mansion, the air was thick with the scent of wealth and excess. Ornate chandeliers hung from the ceiling, casting a golden glow over the luxurious furnishings. A grand staircase swept upwards, and the sounds of laughter and clinking glasses echoed through the halls. Finesse, dressed in a Versace robe and matching slippers, awaited them in the grand foyer. He greeted them with a charming smile, his eyes gleaming with appreciation as he kissed their hands.

"Welcome, Señoritas," Finesse said, turning them in a circle to get a good look. "It must be said, you ladies are the baddest bitchez I've seen in quite some time, forgive my French."

"Thank you," Chrissy replied, her voice smooth and seductive. "We're here to make sure you have an unforgettable night."

"Is that for me?" Finesse asked, taking the bottle of pink champagne from Josephine. "This is sweet. You remembered. My favorite."

"Oh. And this," Chrissy took out the bag of pink cocaine.

Finesse's eyes bubbled when he saw the psychoactive substance. "Tusi," he called the drug by its nickname as he plucked it from Chrissy's fingers. "You girls follow me," he walked away, opening the $600 of champagne, and leading them to his extravagant bedroom.

Chrissy and Josephine exchanged a knowing glance as they entered Finesse's lavish bedroom. It was time to put their plan into action. Chrissy programmed her cellphone to play Jeremih's "All The Time" and propped it against the dresser's mirror. With practiced ease, the girls began to strip and dance for the kingpin, their movements graceful and mesmerizing. Finesse wiped his wet chin as he plopped down on the side of his bed, setting the bottle of champagne on the nightstand. Pulling open the top drawer, he removed a mirror with cocaine residue on it and a neatly rolled one-hundred-dollar bill. He dumped a little more than half the pink cocaine onto the mirror, making six lines with his black American Express credit card.

Finesse snorted up one of the pink lines and its sensation hit him like a missile. He threw his head back blinking his glassy eyes and thumbing his nose. He snorted like a pig to stop from sneezing and wasting the synthetic cocaine. Chrissy and Josephine, topless and wearing G-strings, exchanged glances as they danced provocatively in the kingpin's direction. Finesse had snorted up a second line and looked back up. His vision was obscured and he felt woozy. He thought it was the coke but it was the sleeping agent the girls mixed with it.

Finesse set the mirror with the pink cocaine on the nightstand and got up from the bed, removing his robe. He engaged Chrissy and Josephine in a three-way kiss, groping their asses roughly. The girls slid down his chest, sucking his nipples and slipping their hands down his pants. One stroked his wand to life while the other stimulated his sac. A smile manifested on his lips as the ladies pleased him. He yawned and smacked his lips. His eyelids felt like they had five-pound weights on them.

Finesse fell backward, bouncing off the side of the bed and landing on the floor unconscious. Josephine quickly held two fingers to the side of his neck, checking his pulse and ensuring he was out cold. "This nigga out. Help me get 'em inside the tub so we can remove his eye and get outta here," she grabbed Finesse under his arms as Chrissy approached to take hold of his legs.

***

Once the girls had gotten Finesse inside the jacuzzi-style tub, Josephine fixed a napkin cloth around his neck while Chrissy went to get something. Chrissy returned to the bathroom with one of the bottles of pink champagne, twisting its lower half and pulling it free. The lower half contained a scalpel, a small bottle of rubbing alcohol, and a folded sheet of paper. Chrissy removed the scalpel's casing, squirted some of the alcohol on the surgical instrument, and extended it to Josephine.

Josephine's brows wrinkled as she looked at the scalpel and then Chrissy. "Bitch, what the fuck you tryna gemme that for?"

"So you can cut this nigga's eye out. Now here, girl. We don't have all night," Chrissy shook the scalpel at her.

"Bullshit. You better gone somewhere with that, you've got me fucked up." Josephine spat, looking at her like she was an idiot.

"Nuh unh," Chrissy shook her head. "I put chu onto this lick, so if anyone's hands gonna get bloody, it's gonna be yours."

"Hold up. You didn't tell me you were gonna be makin' up the rules and shit." Josephine twisted her lips and folded her arms across her breasts. "Don't chu think we shoulda discussed this before we agreed to do this job together?"

Right then, Finesse snorted like a warthog and startled the girls. They looked at him with bubble eyes and racing hearts. When they realized he was still asleep from the sedatives they mixed in the pink cocaine, they sighed with relief with their hands over their chest.

"Whew, chile, this nigga scared the hell outta me," Josephine confessed.

"Scared my ass, too," Chrissy admitted. "Now, listen, I'm not tryna be around when this nigga wakes up, so we'll play Rock, Paper, Scissors. The loser has to cut this muthafucka's eye out. Deal?" she extended her hand.

"Deal." Josephine went to shake Chrissy's hand, but she snatched it away. Chrissy noticed she was hiding her hand behind her back, which meant she probably had her fingers crossed.

"Ho, I may live inna small house, but it's far from stupid. Lemme see yo' hand if we gon' do this."

Josephine held up the hand she'd hidden so Chrissy could see it. They played Rock, Paper, Scissors three times before Chrissy eventually won.

"Fuck!" Josephine cussed, swinging her fist in frustration. She hated losing.

Chrissy smirked victoriously and held out the scalpel. Josephine begrudgingly snatched it and kneeled beside Finesse. She watched as Chrissy unfolded the sheet of paper that was inside the bottom half of the champagne bottle. It was handwritten instructions on how to remove an eyeball from someone's socket. Josephine took a couple of deep breaths and leaned closer to the kingpin. Her hand shook like Michael J. Fox's as she tried her best to hold the sharp metal tool still. Chrissy cringed when Josephine sliced into the corner of Finesse's eye and blood skeeted in her face.

***

Josephine placed Finesse's eyeball inside a Rubbermaid bowl of ice and put it inside her purse. Once she and Chrissy finally emerged from the mansion, they found Finesse's security guards lying unconscious on the porch. The girls' lipstick had worked its magic so they'd be knocked out for hours.

Chrissy didn't waste any time hitting up her boo to let him know what was good. Jayvon's cellphone rang twice before he picked it up.

"Mission accomplished," Chrissy gave him the code phrase.

"See you in twenty, Doll," Jayvon replied, then disconnected the call.

Chrissy slipped her cellphone inside her purse and turned to Josephine, who passed her a blunt she'd lit. Chrissy indulged as her girl drove off the grounds of Finesse's mansion to the drop zone.

***

The van navigated the winding road to the safe house, its tires crunched against the gravel, sending pebbles skittering in its wake. The landscape surrounding the property was rugged and untamed, with dense forest stretching as far as the eye could see, providing a natural barrier against prying eyes. Surrounding the perimeter of the house were armed guards standing watch, dressed in black caps and matching fatigues. They were on high alert, their senses attuned to the slightest disturbance in the stillness of the night. Every guard held their post with dedication and was committed to their duty.

As the van approached, the tension among the guards was almost tangible, their hands instinctively tightening around the grips of their assault rifles. They exchanged wary glances, communicating silently with one another as they prepared for any threats to the security of their boss's fortune. But as the van came to a stop and the tinted window slid down, they were relieved to see it was their employer seated in the passenger seat. Their boss, Finesse, was a man of formidable presence and influence to them. Instantly, the guards' hardened faces softened, and they exchanged nods of recognition among themselves.

"How are—" Jayvon, disguised as Finesse, began but cleared his throat. He'd forgotten to sound more like the man he was impersonating. "Excuse me, but how are things tonight?"

"Boring as usual, but you won't getta complaint outta me, jefe, boring is good. I love it," the chief guard, Falco said, adjusting his black cap. The rest of the guards exchanged glances and nods. They didn't mind it being boring because it meant they would be making easy money.

"Amen to that shit," Finesse cracked a grin. "Listen, I brought along some new recruits. They're gonna help me transport my money to a more secure location. Once we wrap things up here, you're free to go on about your night as you please."

The head guard opened the passenger door for Finesse and he stepped out of the van, buttoning his suit jacket. He looked at the guards standing on the post protecting his money. With the firepower they had, he knew he and the gang wouldn't make it out of there alive if their covers were blown.

Chyna and Bag Man, dressed in black caps and fatigues, hopped out of the van cradling their firearms and taking in the scenery. They nodded to the guards like *what's up?* But only got hard stares in return.

"Punk ass muthafuckaz think they're hard," Bag Man whispered in Chyna's ear.

"I second that," Chyna whispered back, keeping his eyes on the opposition.

"If I thought they'd be game, I'd suggest putting away this artillery and throwin' them thangs." Bag Man said, staring the guards down.

"And I'd be standing right beside you, knockin' shit out," Chyna assured him. "We're not here for that though, unc. We're tryna get this schmoney, so play it cool. A'ight?"

"Don't worry. I'm just saying, youngin'," Bag Man told him. "I'm not gonna blow the mission."

"Understood, sir." Falco nodded his understanding to Finesse.

A faint smile tugged at the corners of the Finesse's lips. "Excellent," he said, gaze sweeping over the perimeter of the property, "Alright, gentlemen, let's be on our way," he told Chyna and Bag Man, continuing towards the front door. As they disappeared inside, Falco and the other guards returned to their posts.

***

Inside the house, the atmosphere was tense yet controlled, the air thick with anticipation as Jayvon, Chyna, and Bag Man made their way toward the basement. Here, hidden behind a facade of ordinary items, lay Finesse's most closely guarded secret—a vault containing untold riches.

As he approached the mock furnace, his fingers brushed against the cool metal surface, tracing the hidden mechanism that would grant him access to the treasure he desired. With a soft click, the facade slid away, revealing the imposing bulk of the vault. Jayvon, Chyna, and Augustus stood before a sleek imposing digital vault. Its metallic surface gleamed under the faint glow of the light in the ceiling. Jayvon looked at Chyna and Bag Man, wearing a mixture of determination and apprehension in his eyes.

"This is it, my niggaz," Jayvon said, fingers tracing the smooth contours of the vault. "There's enough money in this bitch to change our lives forever."

"Keep in mind, once we crack this bitch open, we're gonna spend the rest of our lives lookin' over our shoulders." Bag Man informed him.

Chyna nodded in agreement with Bag Man. He knew Finesse wasn't a joke, and by taking his money, he was sure to have every hitta under his command gunning for them.

Jayvon nodded, his eyes fixed on the 4-inch screen above the small keypad adorned the vault's front panel. "True. But we've come too far to turn back now," Jayvon replied, his voice steady despite the flutter of nerves in his chest. He kept getting an eerie feeling Finesse's goons would burst into the room and chop them down.

Throwing caution to the wind, Jayvon unbuckled his belt and unzipped his slacks. He removed a pouch stitched into the inside seams of his pants. He opened the pouch and revealed Finesse's eyeball, perched on a bed of hot ice to keep it fresh and cold.

Jayvon kissed the eyeball. "A'ight, here goes nothing, baby," he said, holding the eyeball up to the 4-inch screen on the side of the vault. A red laser projected from the screen and into the pupil of the eyeball, scanning it for authentic identification. The laser disappeared and a message appeared on the display. *Please, enter your passcode.* Jayvon placed Finesse's eyeball back inside the pouch and went to punch in the passcode the girls gave him. With each press of a button, the tension in the basement grew palpable, until finally, with a soft click, the vault's door opened. Chyna and Bag Man sat their assault rifles against the wall and pushed the vault's door open, revealing its hidden contents. There were blocks and blocks of one-hundred-dollar bills packaged in clear plastic. Jayvon gazed upon the treasure nestled within the vault's depths, heart pounding with exhilaration. Right then, he knew without a doubt, there wasn't a piece of candy in the world that tasted sweeter than victory.

Jayvon, Chyna, and Bag Man stood side by side, bathed in the soft blue glow of the vault's light. They all smiled. In that moment, they had proven that with ingenuity, even the most formidable obstacles could be overcome. Time was of the essence and the fellas didn't have a second to waste. They knew it would take them hours to pack the money inside their duffle bags and load them inside their van, so Jayvon enlisted the men guarding the house to assist them. His request was bold, but the way he saw it, they didn't have any other choice.

CHAPTER TWELVE

"That's the last of 'em," Bag Man announced, smacking the imaginary dirt from his hands. He, Jayvon, Chyna, and Finesse's guards had just finished loading the duffle bags inside the back of the van.

"You guys were a big help." Jayvon grinned from the side of the van. He didn't help load the duffle bags, he watched as the task was performed from the sidelines.

Chyna jumped down from the back of the van. "You ain't never lied, make me feel kinda bad we gotta do this."

Falco frowned and looked at Jayvon. "What is he talkin' about?"

Swifter than the human eye could detect, Jayvon, Chyna and Bag Man drew their guns.

Boc, boc, boc, boc, blocka, blocka, blocka, bop, bop, bop, bop!

Finesse's guards plopped on the ground, bloody and bleeding profusely. Jayvon, Chyna, and Bag Man tossed their warm, smoking guns on the pavement among the guards' bodies. Everyone piled inside the van and Augustus drove away.

***

"Yo, we did that shit, my niggaz!" Jayvon bellowed, smacking the ceiling.

"Yeaaah, we're riiiich, baybeeee!" Chyna bellowed from behind him, doing a funny dance.

"All of this muthafuckin' loot, we got that A-rab moneyyy!" Bag Man kissed the duffle bags of dead presidents. He then kissed the rest of the fellas, making them frown and wipe their faces.

"Say, hoss, next time you pull that shit, I'ma put one in yo' head and toss yo' ass out inna road. Ya hear?" Augustus frowned. He was genuinely pissed.

"Yeah, bruh, you gon' end up bein' my next fight doin' shit like that." Jayvon shook his head, grinning. He knew Bag Man was excited but he wasn't feeling another man kissing him.

"Aww, man, fuck y'all niggaz." Bag Man waved them off.

Augustus suddenly slammed on the brakes, sending everyone bumping around inside the van. Jayvon, Chyna, and Bag stood up wincing and rubbing their heads.

"Say, my G, fuck you hit them brakes like that for?" Bag Man asked.

Augustus kept his eyes on the road, he didn't say a damn thing. Instead, he pointed to something outside of the window. Jayvon, Chyna, and Bag Man looked in the direction he pointed in. There were two men in ski masks with M-16 assault rifles pointed at them. The shorter of the men had a slight muscular build. The taller man had dreadlocks that spilled from the bottom of his ski mask. A van twice the size of the one Jayvon and them rode in was idling behind them.

Jayvon and the boys went to grab the extra guns they had on deck, but the shorter of the men blasted his assault rifle at the dirt, making them throw up their hands.

"Either one of you hoes makes another move, we gon' give the inside of that van a crimson interior. My word to God." the shorter man swore. "A'ight, now, my guy in the flashy ass suit. Keeping one hand up, I want you to use the other to open the door. You got it?" Jayvon nodded his understanding and carried out the command. The shorter man signaled for his partner-in-crime to watch the gang as they exited the van. The taller man, cradling his

M-16, jogged to the back of the van. Using his assault rifle, he motioned for Jayvon and them to get out.

Chyna was the last one out of the van. He kept his eyes on the taller man, looking for anything he could remember him by in case he bumped into him in the streets. Off back, a name and face flashed in his head. He wanted to say something but he feared he'd be shut down if he did.

"Y'all come up here with me," the shorter man ordered. Once the gang stopped in front of him, he motioned for them to lie on the ground with his assault rifle. They obliged. "Yo, B, gag these boys and put some ties on 'em, gang."

The shorter man kept his assault rifle pinned on Jayvon and them while his partner-in-crime fulfilled his request. The shorter man caught Chyna staring at him intensely. He had a feeling he was trying to remember something distinguished about him so he could find out who he was later. Abruptly, the shorter man kicked dirt into Chyna's eyes, blinding him. He balled his face and clenched his jaws, shaking his head like a wet dog.

"Fuck you lookin' at, huh? You want cho top blown off, boy?" The shorter man asked, his sneaker planted on Chyna's head, mashing his face in the dirt.

Jayvon looked at the shorter man hatefully. "Bitch nigga, get cho fuckin' foot off my lil' brother."

"Aaaaah, shut up," the shorter man mimicked Bugs Bunny, kicking Jayvon in the head.

Chyna was pissed off when the dude assaulted his brother. He popped mad shit through the gag in his mouth and struggled to get out of his restraints. The shorter man laughed, thinking he looked like a fish out of water.

The taller man whistled as he peered inside one of the duffle bags and saw all those dead presidents. He climbed inside the back of the van, slid into the driver's seat, and started it up. He swung the van around, put it in reverse, and backed it up to the open door of their van. With the vans being so close together it would be easy to transfer the load from one vehicle to the other.

The taller man, who was Bocka, set his M-16 down on the passenger seat of their van. Keeping on his ski mask, he pulled off his shirt and exposed the bulletproof vest he wore underneath. He knew he would work up one hell of a sweat pulling the duffle bags from one van to the other. And he didn't want to get his clothes sweaty and smelling.

By the time Bocka had gotten done moving the money, he was sweating like he'd run a marathon for some charity. He pulled Jayvon's van away from the one he and the shorter man drove there. Slamming the driver's door shut, he jogged to the van's opposite side and waved over D'Anthony (the shorter man) so they could leave.

D'Anthony fired at the front tire on the driver's side of the van where they'd placed the duffle bags of cash. The tire hissed as it released pressure and leaned to one side.

"Well, my niggaz, it's been real," D'Anthony saluted the gang and retreated to the van, hopping into the passenger seat. Bocka started up the van and zipped down the road, leaving a cloud of dirt behind.

"Fuuuuuck!" Jayvon screamed and slammed his forehead against the ground repeatedly. He watched the back of the van until it disappeared down the road and tears slid down his cheeks.

Jayvon was heartbroken. Not only had the jack boys taken his fortune, they'd taken his father's life because if Draco didn't get his bread his old man was as good as dead.

***

Beneath the cloak of darkness, a white cargo van backed into the backyard of a house. Bocka and D'Anthony hopped out of the cargo van and opened its doors. Dolph and a fat nigga named Chunky came out of the backdoor of the house. Dolph, pistol in hand, stood watch at the front of the cargo van making sure there weren't any Money Hungry Demons lurking.

Bocka, D'Anthony, and Chunky removed duffle bag after duffle bag from the back of the cargo van and carried them through the backdoor. By the time they'd completed the task, they were all hot and sweaty, but eager to count the spoils from their labor.

***

Dolph, Bocka, D'Anthony, and Chunky stood inside the kitchen looking at the money they'd stolen. Although they were all seasoned, hardened criminals, there wasn't a man among those gathered who could stop the smiles from forming on their lips. A single tear slid down Dolph's cheek and he wiped it away. In all his years of hustling, stealing, killing, and jacking he'd never seen a sight as beautiful as this one. He knew he'd been playing in a game with higher stakes than he could imagine, but this lick made everything worth it.

Once D'Anthony and Bocka received their cut from the Finesse lick, they shook up with Dolph and Chunky and left the house. Their last task of the night was to burn the cargo van they'd used to commit their transgressions, and then they could be on their way home. Bocka had too many glasses of Jamaican rum punch at the count-up house and now he had to take a leak. He tried holding it until they reached their destination, but his bladder felt like it was going to explode. He drove over to the side of the road and turned off the van. He was about to hop out to take a piss when he saw D'Anthony put something in his ears. He started to mind his business but his curiosity got the best of him.

"Wut are doze? New AirPods?" Bocka asked.

"Nah, these ain't no AirPods, Rasta," D'Anthony laughed.

Bocka frowned. "Den wut da fuck are dey den?"

"Ear plugs," D'Anthony scowled, upped his gun, and shot Bocka in the temple. His blood and brain fragments splattered against the window and the ceiling, dripping. He lay against the driver's window, eyes wide and mouth open. His dreadlocks were so bloody they looked like Flamin' Hot Cheetos.

D'Anthony removed his earplugs and wiped the blood from his face. Hopping out of the cargo van, he looked around to make sure there wasn't anyone watching him as he opened its doors. It took a while but he managed to transfer the duffle bags from the van to his Denali, which he'd hidden in the woods. Sometime later, he eased out onto the road and drove back toward the count-up spot.

As D'Anthony raced up the road, he thought back to how he ended up in his position in the first place.

***

Dolph made his way through the corridors of D'Anthony's building. The pungent smell of mildew and decay assaulted his senses, the dwelling was a far cry from the pristine luxury afforded to him. He knocked on D'Anthony's apartment door and he opened it.

D'Anthony's eyes widen in surprise at his unexpected visitor. "Uh, what up, Dolph?" he asked.

"What up, young king?" Dolph said, shaking up with him. "You gon' letta nigga in or what?"

"Oh, my bad, big homie. Come in," he said, stepping aside to allow him entry.

"Are we alone?" Dolph asked.

"Yeah. MaDuke's gon' grocery shoppin' with the twins and lil' sis."

Dolph's eyes swept over the faded wallpaper and threadbare furniture, his expression unreadable. "I have a proposition for you, youngin'," he began, voice low and laced with intrigue. After he'd taken in D'Anthony's apartment he knew he'd be willing to do whatever he asked to get his hands on some money.

As Dolph outlined his offer, D'Anthony's eyes flickered with greed at the promise of an easy twenty grand and membership to the King of Thieves. The opportunity to keep tabs on Chyna, another young man who had become like a brother to him, was too enticing to resist. Yet, a shadow of doubt lingered in the recesses of his mind.

"Chyna's entangled in a dangerous game, D' Anthony. He owes a debt to these Spanish niggaz, and I needa ensure my interests are safeguarded when he settles it," Dolph explained, his words carrying an ominous weight. He knew Chyna and Jayvon would go hard to get the money they owed to Draco, and no matter what, he wanted to make sure the Kings of Thieves got their issue.

A shiver of apprehension crossed D'Anthony's mind, but the allure of money clouded his judgment. With a hesitant nod, he agreed to Dolph's terms, and they shook up.

***

Unbeknownst to Chyna, he'd inadvertently pocket-dialed D'Anthony, unleashing a cascade of incriminating details that echoed through the receiver. D'Anthony's eyes widened as he listened intently, his world tilting on its axis as he heard the nefarious plan to rob Finesse of a staggering $150,000,000.

D'Anthony pressed the mute button on his cellphone so Chyna wouldn't hear anything on his end. Grabbing an ink pen, he quickly jotted down the crucial details of the heist – the date and the time – ensuring he had all the necessary information.

CHAPTER THIRTEEN

The dining room was heavy with tension as D'Anthony recounted the intricate details of the impending heist to Dolph, whose eyes gleamed with excitement. "We gotta golden opportunity here, big homie," D'Anthony began, his voice laced with anticipation. "We can intercept the robbery and claim this nigga Finesse's fortune for ourselves."

Dolph's mind whirled with possibilities as he formulated a plan. "A'ight, youngin', I'm tasking you and Bocka with this," he declared, his tone decisive. "You'll tail King Chyna and his cohorts from his brother's place to wherever this Finesse keeps his loot stashed." Bocka nodded in agreement. He was all for it. "I'll bring in King Chunky to hold us down at the count-up spot."

"A'ight, bet," D'Anthony said, shaking up with Dolph and then Bocka.

Dolph and Bocka watched as D'Anthony walked out of the house. The door clicked shut, leaving Dolph and Bocka alone in the dining room. Dolph's calculating gaze locked onto Bocka, a silent understanding passed between them as they stood on the precipice of deceit. "We've been lining the pockets of my brother and his brethren far too long, Bocka," Dolph said, voice a low murmur of conspiracy. "I think it's time we kept the spoils for ourselves and split it between us."

Bocka's eyes widened with avarice, a greedy smile curling his lips. "Yew mean tree ways. Ya forgettin' 'bout thee liddle wun?"

Dolph's expression darkened, his features becoming demon-like. "I haven't forgotten about 'em," he retorted icily. "The lil' nigga may have cut us in, but we're gonna cut 'em out."

"Me dunt have no problem wit dat. More for us."

Unbeknownst to him and Dolph, D'Anthony had been eavesdropping from the other side of the door. His heart was heavy with the weight of their deception. The revelation struck him like lightning and shattered the fragile trust he had placed in who he thought were his allies.

***

I may be young, but I stay on my toes. That's how I got the drop on y'all Gumps, D'Anthony thought as he parked his truck outside the count-up house and turned off its engine. He slipped his hands inside a pair of black leather gloves, picked his .45 up from his lap, and screwed a silencer on it. Hopping out, he tucked his gun inside his waistband and knocked on the front door of the count-up house.

"Who is it?" Chunky called out.

"It's King D," D'Anthony replied as he glanced back at the street. Anyone looking would be able to tell he was anxious.

"Say, Dolph, it's that lil' nigga that was here with Bocka." D'Anthony overheard Chunky tell Dolph.

"See what the young king wants," Dolph told him.

"What chu want, my nigga?" Chunky asked.

"I think I left my shades in there, B," D'Anthony said. "I may have forgotten them inside the bathroom or the kitchen. I paid $1,500 for them shits."

"Nigga said he left his sunglasses in here somewhere," Chunky reported to Dolph.

"Well, let the lil' homie in so we can finish piecing up this loot," Dolph replied.

The next thing D'Anthony knew the locks were coming undone and Chunky was pulling open the front door. Chunky's face was scrunched and his stubby fingers were wrapped around a Tec-9. He waved D'Anthony in with his weapon and locked the door behind him. The moment Chunky turned around he was met with the silencer of a .45. His eyes bubbled and he gasped. His face exploded and speckles of blood clung to D'Anthony's face. Chunky fell to the floor so hard the entire living room shook. Dolph thought it was an earthquake. He wasn't too sure so he picked up his gun from the kitchen table, mashed out his blunt, and jumped to his feet.

"Yo, Chunky, was that an earthquake, or did you fall?" Dolph laughed. He expected Chunky to retort with a funny insult like he always did but his clowning went unanswered. Dolph's eyebrows dipped and his nose scrunched. He had a feeling something was up so he started around the kitchen table. "Yo, Chunky, you goo—"

Dolph was cut short by the sudden appearance of D'Anthony. He upped his gun and fingered its trigger like it was a clit. Dolph's face balled up in agony as the hot bullets seared his chest. He dropped his gun and fell awkwardly to the floor. Coughing up globs of blood, he crawled toward the gun he'd lost in the fall. D'Anthony watched him from the door for a moment before he casually strolled toward him. Dolph took the gun into his hand. D'Anthony kneeled and looked him in the eyes as he lifted his piece.

"Now what do you plan to do with that?" D'Anthony asked. Dolph was about to shoot him in the face when he suddenly shoved his .45 under his chin and pulled the trigger. A bullet ripped through the top of Dolph's skull, sending brain fragments and particles of meat flying everywhere. His head dropped to the floor. His eyes stared up at the ceiling while his mouth hung open.

"Long live the king," D'Anthony said, walking out of the kitchen. He returned with a bed sheet, placed all the money from the lick at the center of it, and tied it up. He tried hoisting the sheet over his shoulder but found it too heavy.

Looks like I'ma just have to drag this bitch outta here, D'Anthony thought. He drugged the sheet out of the house and struggled to place it inside the van. Slamming the doors closed, he wiped his sweaty forehead and smacked imaginary dust from his hands.

With a job well done, D'Anthony jumped back behind the wheel of his SUV and cranked it up. He took the designer shades he claimed to have left at Dolph's spot from the sun visor, slipped them back on, and zipped up the block. His vehicle pulsated with the late great Nipsey Hussle's "Succa-Proof" pumping from its speakers.

***

The sun was coming up by the time Jayvon and the gang crossed back within the city's limits. Augustus had to piss, so he planned to drive to a Publix that had been shut down for quite some time. The entire ride back home Chrissy had been blowing up Jayvon's cellphone, wondering where he was and if the heist was successful. Jayvon refused to say anything over the jack so they made plans for her and Josephine to meet them at Publix.

When Chrissy and Josephine drove inside Publix's parking lot, a sense of unease settled over them as they spotted Jayvon pacing the ground, smoking a cigarette. Bag Man and Chyna looked defeated as they stood beside their van, sharing a bottle of tequila. Instantly, Chrissy felt something was wrong. She and Josephine exchanged worried glances and hopped out of the car.

Jayvon saw them approaching, dropped his cigarette at his foot, and mashed it out. He loosened his tie and looked up at them with sorrowful eyes, appearing both disappointed and defeated. Figuring he should put it out there and get it over with, he came at them straight up. "We got juxed," he said, with a shaky voice. "Two masked niggaz with choppas took everythang we took from Finesse. They didn't leave us with one goddamn dime." he punched the side of the van, making a slight dent in it. "We had it too. We had it all. Fuck."

Chrissy stepped forward, placing a comforting hand on Jayvon's shoulder. "It's okay," she told him. "We'll figure this out."

Josephine's face wrinkled as he clenched her jaws. She stared at Jayvon with anger in her eyes. "Aaah, this some bullshit, bro! Y'all tryna play a bitch, and keep all the money."

Josephine shoved Bag Man out of the way and yanked open the van's doors. She searched the vehicle from top to bottom and didn't find any money. Frustrated, she threw her head back and screamed like someone was stabbing her to death. "Aaaaaaaaaaaaaah!"

Everyone looked at each other like *This bitch is crazy.*

Josephine jumped down from the van and marched toward Jayvon. She'd gotten within three feet of him when Chrissy slid between them.

"Mind your mouth, Joe, this is my man you comin' at." Chrissy frowned. "We've been friends for quite some time now, and I'd hate to have to take it there." she rolled up her sleeves and clenched her fists. Shorty was fully prepared to throw hands behind Jayvon. She knew he'd never let a nigga disrespect her, so she wasn't about to let a bitch come at him sideways.

Chyna and Bag Man tried to interject. "Yo, lil' mama, you wildin' for nothin'. It was a botched lick, didn't nobody come home with nothin'." Bag Man insisted.

Josephine wasn't trying to hear that shit. "That's some bullshit. What kinda fool do y'all take me for? Hell, I've been in the streets practically my whole life. I know when niggaz are tryna finesse me." she spat, glaring at them.

Chrissy stepped in to defend Jayvon. "Josephine, my man, and our friends don't have a reason to lie. Ain't nobody tryna run game on you for that money."

Josephine's anger got the best of her, and before Chrissy could say anything else, she swung at her. Chrissy stumbled backward but quickly regained her equilibrium, rushing Josephine. Feigning a punch, she kicked Josephine in the stomach, doubling her over. Chrissy tackled her to the ground, straddling her and raining blows on her face until Jayvon and Bag Man pulled her off, kicking and screaming.

"Lemme go! Y'all lemme go! This ho got the nerve to try to take a swing at me." Chrissy roared like a lioness defending its cubs.

Josephine scrambled back to her feet, wiping her bloody nose and mouth. "You got that, but this ain't over, bitch. It's far from over." she retreated to her car, started it up, and sped out of the parking lot.

"What the hell's goin' on over here?" Augustus asked as he walked across the parking lot, buckling his belt with his gun in his hand. He was pissing on the side of the building when he heard the girls arguing.

"Shorty didn't take the bad news so well," Jayvon told Augustus. He and Chyna were examining Chrissy's busted knuckles when gunshots rang out.

Bowl, blowl, blowl, blowl!

Everyone dropped to the asphalt, looking in the direction the shots came from. They saw Josephine steering her car with one hand while the other held her gun out of the driver's window.

"Betta grow eyes in the back of yo' head, ho, 'cause it's on now. Believe that!" she shouted, pulling her gun back inside her whip, and peeling out of the parking lot like a speed demon.

Augustus got up and ran over to the space Josephine sped away from. Kneeling, he extended his gun with both hands and returned fire.

Blocka, blocka, blocka, blocka!

Augustus stood back up, staring at Josephine's car until it was out of the parking lot. He spat on the ground. "Crazy ass bitch."

Jayvon got up from the ground and helped Chrissy to her feet. "You a'ight, ma?" he asked, concern etched on his face. She nodded. "How 'bout y'all? Y'all good?"

Chyna and Bag Man nodded. "Yeah, we're good."

Jayvon looked at Augustus, inquiring about his well-being. "OG?"

Augustus checked his clip and smacked it back inside his gun. He looked at Jayvon, nodding. "I'm as good as it gets, youngin'."

Chrissy winced, clenching and unclenching her blood-stained knuckles. "As if we don't already have enough to worry about, here comes one more," she shook her head. Jayvon threw his arm around her shoulders and kissed the side of her head.

CHAPTER FOURTEEN

Finesse woke up in his jacuzzi tub wincing, his left eye aching. Groaning, he reached up to touch his face, only to feel a strange emptiness where his eye should have been. Panic surged through him as he looked around the bathroom, calling out for the strippers he had hired for the night, Josephine and Chrissy. The only response was the echo of his own.

"Josephine? Chrissy? Where the hell are you?" Finesse shouted, his voice laced with confusion and pain. Grimacing, he climbed out of the tub, his legs shaky. He stumbled over to the bathroom mirror and froze, horror washing over him as he stared at his reflection. His left eye was gone, the socket a gruesome void. Blood and water dripped from his face, and he felt a wave of nausea.

"What the—who did this?" Finesse said under his breath, mind spinning. He dashed through his mansion, calling out for Josephine and Chrissy, but there was no sign of them. The mansion was eerily silent. He grabbed his gun from his bedside drawer and ran outside, where he found his security guards just starting to wake up, groggily and disoriented.

"What happened?" one of the guards mumbled, struggling to stand.

"You tell me!" Finesse barked like an angry chihuahua. "Where are Josephine and Chrissy?"

The guards looked at each other, bewildered. "We don't know. The last thing we remember, we were at our posts, and then everything went black."

Finesse's heart pounded as he rushed inside to check the surveillance footage. He fast-forwarded through the recordings, his anxiety growing with each passing second. Finally, he saw it: Josephine and Chrissy were the ones who drugged him and the guards. They hadn't taken anything from the mansion, but he knew better. He knew what they were after.

"Shit," he shouted, his thoughts turning to his fortune, stored in a heavily guarded house out in the middle of nowhere. "The money..." he picked up his burner cellphone and placed a call.

***

Finesse tried contacting his chief guard, but he didn't answer. He hit up his second in command and he didn't answer either. Panic turned to cold determination as he gathered a group of his remaining men and drove out to the safe house. The drive was tense, every minute stretching into an eternity. When they finally arrived, the sight that greeted them was worse than Finesse had feared. The guards who had been assigned to protect his fortune lay dead, their bullet-riddled bodies scattered around the property. The vault where he kept his money had been cleaned out as well.

Finesse stared at the carnage, his heart racing like those drivers in NASCAR. He had been played, and he felt stupid.

"Search the area," he ordered, voice tight with anger. "Find clues, anything that might tell us where they went."

As his men began to scour the property, Finesse stood by the empty vault, seething. The strippers had been a distraction, a means to get to his fortune. They had taken everything from him, and he was left with nothing but rage and a thirst for revenge.

"Pinche morenos," he murmured, balling his fists. "I'll find them and when I do, they'll pay for this."

***

Finesse's men combed through the property, but they didn't find anything. One of his men, a stocky dude with a curly flattop named Rip, approached Finesse, shaking his head.

"Jefe, whoever did this vanished without a trace," Rip reported, his voice heavy with defeat.

In a fit of anger, Finesse snatched an assault rifle from one of his men and sprayed the dead bodies of his guards. Their blood misted the air and pooled underneath them. He turned his fury on the trees, blasting them apart, pieces of bark flying at him. He narrowed his eyes and kept shooting until the assault rifle clicked empty. Then he tossed it back to the guard he'd taken it from. After blowing off steam, he took a moment to gather himself and addressed his men.

"Those whores have taken everything from me," Finesse began. "My eye, my men, my money. This one is personal, I'm gonna crush those bitchez like the cockroaches they are." He looked at his reflection in the window of the black Jeep he had been driven there in. His left eye was dressed with gauze and covered with bandaging that wrapped around his head. "No one crosses me and gets away with it."

Finesse was ready to unleash the full fury of his wrath on everyone who stole his bread.

"Tell me what chu want done, jefe, and I'll do it," Rip swore.

Finesse turned around to Rip, looking at him with his good eye.

That night
Blat!

Earthquake flew through the entrance of Club Big Daddy, landing on his back, and bleeding from a hole in his forehead. Finesse's goons, a mix of ruthless and ready men with grim faces, pushed their way through the terrified crowd, flipping tables and roughing up patrons and employees alike. "Where are Josephine and Chrissy?" Rip barked at anyone who dared to make eye contact. Fear spread like wildfire as the goons made their way through the place, leaving a trail of frightened and bruised people in their wake.

***

Big Daddy, heart racing, ran inside his office and locked the door. Realizing the gravity of the situation, he grabbed his piece from his desk drawer. His hands trembled slightly as he loaded his pistol, but he forced himself to stay focused. He picked up his cellphone and hit up Chrissy, hoping she would answer.

"For the last time, Big Daddy, I'm not coming back to work at the club," Chrissy's voice came through the line, clearly annoyed.

"Chris, listen to me," Big Daddy said urgently, loading the clip in his pistol. "Finesse's men are here, tearing the place apart looking for you and Joe. You needa pack your shit and get the fuck outta dodge. You hear me?"

"What about you?" Chrissy asked, panic creeping into her voice.

"I'll be fine, don't worry about me," Big Daddy lied.

Boom!

A goon kicked open the office door violently. Big Daddy didn't hesitate to open fire. He dropped him, but more of Finesse's goons spilled through the door. The room filled with the deafening sound of gunfire as Big Daddy took down one goon after another. Chrissy could hear the chaos over the phone, her heart sinking with every shot.

Blocka, blocka, blocka!

Blatatatatatatat!

"Big Daddy!" Chrissy screamed.

Finesse's goons were like roaches. For everyone Big Daddy killed, another one took its place. They just kept coming. Big Daddy was outnumbered and outgunned. Despite his valiant effort, he was eventually overwhelmed. The last thing Chrissy heard was the sound of Big Daddy's gun clicking empty, followed by a final barrage of gunfire.

Rip picked up Big Daddy's cellular, hearing Chrissy's frantic breathing on the other end. "Who is this?" he growled, voice cold and menacing.

Chrissy was too terrified to answer. Rip smirked, realizing who it must be. "You bitchez fucked up. Now you're dead. You're dead!" Chrissy disconnected the call, and he tossed Big Daddy's cell aside. He turned around to another goon who was busy rummaging through Big Daddy's desk, tossing papers and knickknacks aside until he found a small black book. He opened the book and flipped through its pages quickly. He found Josephine and Chrissy's phone numbers and addresses.

"Got their addresses, let's get the fuck outta here," the goon announced, snatching out the pages containing the information they needed. Rip and the goon fled Big Daddy's office, hearing police sirens wailing in the distance.

***

Unbeknownst to Chrissy, Jayvon and the gang were standing behind her while she talked to Big Daddy. Sensing something was wrong, Jayvon and the gang raided his cache of guns. By the time they came back to the living room, Chrissy had hung up on Rip.

"What's the matter, Doll?" Jayvon asked, taking her into his arms. She cried against his chest.

"Finesse's men came through the club looking for me and Joe," Chrissy said, voice cracking emotionally. "They-they killed Big Daddy…Oh, my God. I've gotta warn Joe." she scrolled through her contacts for Josephine's number.

***

Josephine sat at the head of the dinner table, watching her five children devour their meal with the kind of enthusiasm only kids could muster. Her baby daddy, Marcus, was in the middle of a funny story, making everyone laugh. Just as she was about to take a bite of her own food, her cellphone rang. The screen displayed Chrissy's name. Josephine hesitated, a frown creasing her forehead.

"Don't you think you should answer that?" Marcus said, pausing his story. "Maybe she changed her mind and wants to give you your cut of that money."

Josephine gave it a quick thought and picked up the cellphone. "Hello?"

"Josephine!" Chrissy's voice was frantic. "You need to take your family and get out of the house right now! Finesse is after you!"

Before Josephine could respond, the front door burst open, and goons armed with AR-15s with suppressors stormed inside. Marcus sprang up from the table, but a short burst of gunfire sent him crashing back into his chair, his body lifeless.

The children screamed, their wails piercing the air. Josephine stood frozen, her mind unable to process the horror unfolding before her. One of the goons speed-walked up to her and punched her in the face, knocking her out cold. She crumpled to the floor, her cellphone lying beside her with Chrissy's voice still frantically calling her name.

***

Josephine sat gagged and duct-taped to a chair inside a spacious bathroom. Her eyes are glassy and pink from crying, with snot sliding out of her nostrils. Two of Finesse's goons stand guard on either side of the bathroom door, armed with AR-15s, faces stern and unyielding.

Finesse strolled into the bathroom whistling, the sharp click of his Italian leather shoes echoing off the tile. He removed his suit jacket and carefully draped it over the edge of the bathtub. He rolled up his sleeves and took a look at his reflection in the bathroom mirror, fixing his hair. The eye patch lying over his right eye socket was a grim reminder of the brutal lengths to which Josephine and Chrissy had gone to steal his money.

Finesse kneeled in front of Josephine and tilted his head slightly, studying her. "You know you have the most beautiful children I have ever laid eyes on," he said tenderly, stealing a look at her five terrified kids. "I'd hate to do to them this awful thing I have in mind, but I will if you don't tell me where my money is." He allowed his gaze to linger on her so she'd know he meant business and he wasn't fucking around.

Josephine, her voice muffled by the gag, tried to speak, tears sliding down her cheeks. "I swear, I don't know! I didn't get a dime of your money, not one red cent. I was told that there were masked men...masked men came and jacked Chrissy's guy and his crew for it. I swear!"

Finesse's eyebrows slanted and his nose scrunched. "I'm not tryna hear that shit," he said coldly. He nodded to one of the goons, who grabbed one of Josephine's boys by the collar of his shirt and dragged him over to him. The child's eyes were wide with fear. He screamed as he struggled against the goon's grip.

"Please, no! Don't hurt 'em!" Josephine screamed, her voice cracking with desperation.

Ignoring her, Finesse grabbed the boy by the back of his neck and forced his head into the bathtub filled with water. The kid's arms swung wildly, and his legs kicked frantically, water splashing onto the floor. Josephine thrashed in her chair, screaming incoherently through the gag, but the duct tape held her firmly in place.

The child's movements slowed, then ceased, and the last bubbles rose to the water's surface. Finesse pulled him out and laid him on his back, his small, lifeless body was a heart-wrenching sight.

The remaining children scream in terror, their cries echoing in the spacious bathroom. Two of them ran to Josephine, hugging her tightly, their little bodies shaking with sobs. The other two, a little boy and a girl, attempt to escape, but the goons catch them effortlessly.

Finesse grabbed the little girl, her screams pierced the air as she was dragged to the bathtub. He forced her head under the water, maintaining eye contact with Josephine. "Tell me where Chrissy is," he demanded, with a low and menacing voice.

"I don't know! Please, please stop!" Josephine pleaded, her voice breaking.

When the poor girl's struggle ended, Finesse placed her beside her brother on the floor. Turning to Josephine, he asked again, "Where. Is. Chrissy?"

"I don't know! I swear, I don't know!" she cried, voice raw with agony.

Frustrated, Finesse grabbed another child, holding them underwater until their struggles ceased. He repeated this horrific act, demanding information with each life he took, but Josephine's answer never changed.

Finally, all of Josephine's children lie dead on the bathroom floor. Josephine's cheeks are soaked with tears. Her eyes are vacant and filled with despair. Thinking she might be ready to talk, Finesse rips the duct tape from her lips. She started softly singing "The Mockingbird Song," her voice barely a whisper.

"Hello? Is anyone home?" Finesse asked, snapping his fingers and waving a hand before her eyes. Josephine was so lost in her grief that she didn't respond.

Disappointed, Finesse blew his breath and shook his head. Rising to his feet, he retrieved his suit jacket and slipped it on.

"What chu want us to do with this bitch, boss?" one of the goons asked Finesse as he walked past him, heading out of the door.

"Leave her be, she isn't worth killing at this point," Finesse replied.

Finesse's goons followed him out of the bathroom, leaving Josephine with the bodies of her lifeless children. She continued to sing long after Finesse and his goons were gone.

Mama's gonna buy you a diamond ring.

And if that diamond ring turns brass,

Mama's gonna buy you a looking glass.

And if that looking glass gets broke...

Somewhere in the house, Josephine's cellphone rang repeatedly.

CHAPTER FIFTEEN

Chrissy paced the floor calling Josephine back to back, but never getting an answer. Chyna, Bag Man, and Augustus lounged around with their assault rifles. Jayvon, holding his assault rifle at his shoulder, peered out of the curtains looking like Malcolm X.

Jayvon turned away from the curtains, holding his weapon over his shoulder. "Doll, shorty, still not answering the jack?"

Chrissy shook her head, no. She tried calling Josephine one more time and got sent straight to voicemail. Frustrated, she sat down at the dining room table and set her cellphone aside.

"Look, if they knew where shorty laid her head, then they most likely got that info from off ol' boy's books," Jayvon told her, caressing her hair lovingly. "What address does dude have on you at the club?"

Chrissy looked up at Jayvon as he continued to caress her hair. "Big Daddy has Bartise's address."

"You think Finesse's goons will slide there?" Jayvon asked.

Chrissy thought about it for a moment before answering. "Baby, we hit his ass for $150,000,000. That's a lot of fucking money," she said. "If a nigga gotchu for a purse that size, wouldn't you be everywhere you thought he would be to get it back?"

***

Four black-on-black Jeep Wranglers were parked outside of Bartise's mansion. Finesse's goons, mean mugging, stood around the vehicles holding assault rifles. Rip, the goons' leader, stood on the hood of his Jeep. He had his assault rifle hoisted on his shoulder and a megaphone held to his mouth.

***

Bartise, Purp, and Stutter-Box, who wore bulletproof vests, stood inside the armory loading their weapons. As they prepared for a possible confrontation, they listened to Rip over the megaphone.

"...All we want is the girl, so if she's in there, I suggest you send her out now!" Rip's voice rang from outside to inside the mansion.

Unbeknownst to them, Wild Child entered the armory in a wife beater and gray Dickie's he'd cut into shorts. He started over in Bartise and the gangs' direction.

Bartise frowned when he saw him approaching. "What are you doing in here?"

"Sounds like that fool outside is lookin' for trouble," Wild Child said. "This is my home now so I'ma help hold it down. Toss me one of those vests and a stick."

"Notta chance, youngin'," Bartise replied, cocking a round in his modified Tec-9. "You're a multimillion-dollar investment. I lose you, and my money goes down the drain. I can't have that."

These rich guys are all the same. All I am is a money tree to them, Wild Child thought. *I swear on my life, as soon as I meet my family, I'm done with this fighting shit.*

Bartise took a bulletproof vest from the armory, passing it to Wild Child. "Here, put this on. Go back to your room and stay low to the floor, in case shit gets crazy." He strapped the body armor on Wild Child, looking like a father dressing his son. "There you go." he clapped his shoulder.

"Outta the way, junior," Purp said, bumping past Wild Child.

"Y—yeah. Fuck—fuck out the—out the way," Stutter-Box bumped past Wild Child as well.

"Come on, Wild," Bartise nudged Wild Child, leaving out the armory behind his goons.

Wild Child stayed behind for a moment before heading out of the armory.

***

Purp and Stutter-Box stepped out on the mansion's porch and pinned their AR-15s on two of Finesse's goons. Bartise walked out next, Tec-9 in one hand and a megaphone in the other.

"Chrissy no longer takes up residence here. She's been gone for quite some time," Bartise's voice rang through the megaphone. "Now, I suggest you fools put feet to ground and get the fuck outta here 'fore shit gets messy."

"The only way we're leaving here is with Chrissy in tow, so if shit has to get messy then so be it," Rip's voice rang out of the megaphone. He'd promised himself when he'd gotten there he wasn't leaving unless he had Chrissy or knew where she could be found. He refused to report back to Finesse empty-handed.

"Messy it is then!" Bartise replied through the megaphone before throwing it aside. He unsheathed his cobra-head cane, revealing a sword.

Throwing his megaphone aside, Rip hoisted up his assault rifle and jumped to the ground. He was prepared to die in the name of his mission.

***

D'Anthony wiped the sweat from his brow as he finished burying the majority of the cash in the backyard of an old condemned house. It was a place he had once pointed out to Chyna while they were driving, a perfect hideout for his loot. Satisfied with his work, he covered the buried spot with leaves, carved an X into the tree looming over it, and drove to the Red Hook projects.

As he entered the familiar territory of Red Hook, he spotted four knuckleheads he used to terrorize the neighborhood with. They were smoking and drinking, lounging against a graffiti-covered wall.

"Yo, D!" one of them called out, exhaling a cloud of smoke.

D'Anthony walked up to them, a confident grin on his face. "What's good, son?" he greeted, shaking up with all of them.

"Same old, same old," Marlo replied, passing a blunt. "Where you been though, B?"

"You know a nigga got motion, I've been handling business," D'Anthony replied, reaching into his knapsack. He pulled out stacks of money, handing each of his four homies forty bands. "Here, that's for y'all niggaz, don't worry about hittin' me back either. It's onna love." he tapped his fist against his chest.

The man's eyes lit up like kids on Christmas getting the toy they wanted as they took the cash. A couple of them held up one of the bills to the light to check its authenticity while the other two acted like they were calling each other on money phones.

"Damn, my nigga D, where'd you get all this?" Hill, another one of the crew, asked.

"Don't worry about that," D'Anthony said, voice low and commanding. "Look, I'm leveling up in these streets, which means money, power, and haters, so the kid is gon' need soldiers by his side. Y'all niggaz with me?"

The four young men exchanged glances, their eyes widening at the sight of the cash. "We're witchu, bro," Marlo said, nodding eagerly.

"We ride or die," Jay added.

They dapped up and hugged, sealing their agreement. D'Anthony felt a surge of power and anticipation. He walked away with an easy smile on his lips, holding one strap of the knapsack over his shoulder.

Yeah, the game is gonna be mine.

***

D'Anthony made his way to his building, taking the elevator up. The strong smell of urine assaulted his senses as he stepped inside, but he ignored it and focused on his mission. He entered the cramped apartment wearing a mask of seriousness. he shared with his mother and siblings. The familiar sounds of the neighborhood—distant police sirens, barking dogs, and the hum of traffic—filled the background, creating a contrast to the tension in the living room.

D'Anthony's mother, Trisha, a petite woman wearing big glasses that made her look nerdy, sang softly as she moved around in the kitchen, grabbing different seasons and spices from the cabinets. The delicious smell of Jambalaya, curry chicken, and bread pudding filled the air. This was D'Anthony's favorite meal and dessert, but he had to stay focused on the situation.

"Ma, we've gotta get outta dodge," D'Anthony said, voice firm but tinged with urgency.

Trisha removed the bread pudding from the oven and placed it on top of the stove. Removing her overmitts, she turned to her oldest child, confusion, and concern etched on her face. Her usually warm and welcoming eyes, now reflected a growing anxiety. "Why? What's happened?"

D'Anthony sighed, rubbing the back of his neck. "I've done something bad, and I may or may not have some people after me." He saw the worry consume her eyes and quickly added, "You, Jericho, Terrio and LeeLee needa leave tomorrow morning. You'll spend the night at Aunt Penny's tonight. It will be safer there."

Trisha searched his eyes for answers, worry lines around her mouth deepening. "W—what about you? What are you going to do?"

"Don't worry about me, Ma. I'll be straight," D'Anthony reassured her. He was confident he had everything under control, but in case shit went left, he wanted his family out of harm's way. "Have one of the boys look up some plane tickets to Chicago. Don't worry about the cost, 'cause I'm footin' the bill." When he said this Trisha knew he'd done something that landed him a bunch of money, but she was afraid to ask what exactly that was. "When you touch down, grab a hotel or whatever, getta rental, and find us a new spot to stay. I'll be out there in a couple of weeks after I tie up some loose ends here."

D'Anthony saw fear and concern in his mother's eyes, the way her lips trembled. She tried to be strong, but the tears burst from her eyes. D'Anthony stepped closer, gently wiping the tears from her cheeks. Her skin felt soft and familiar, a comforting reminder of the love and support she had always given him. He kissed her softly on the cheek, the warmth of her skin contrasting with the cold dread in his heart. "Everything's going to be okay, OG. I promise."

D'Anthony reached into his knapsack and pulled out several stacks of money, placing them on the kitchen table. The crisp bills formed a small mountain of cash. His mother's eyes widened in shock, her gaze shifting from the money to his face and back again.

"Ma, I want you to finda nice four-bedroom house in The Chi for us to live in," D'Anthony said, his voice steady. "Buy some nice furniture, too. Make it feel like home." He took her hands in his, feeling the familiar roughness of her hardworking fingers. "I'ma have my guys, Jay and Hill, make sure y'all get out there safely. They're good niggaz. I trust them."

Trisha's mother nodded slowly, still processing everything. The weight of the situation hung heavy in the air, the tension almost palpable. The kitchen, usually a place of warmth and comfort, felt like a staging ground for a hasty retreat. D'Anthony hugged her tightly, feeling her cling to him as if trying to hold on to a sense of normalcy in the chaos.

"I love you, Ma," he whispered, voice choked with emotion. "I'm doing this for us, to make sure we're good."

She held him a moment longer before pulling back, her eyes searching his. "I love you too, baby. Just... be careful. Please."

D'Anthony kissed her on the cheek and headed towards the bedroom he shared with his brothers. Upon entering the bedroom, he found the twins playing Madden on the PS5 he bought them. Though they were happy to see him, the game system had their attention. D'Anthony greeted his siblings with their exclusive handshake. He watched them play the game for a minute before offering the twin, who had just turned the football over some supportive words.

"Head up, chest out, young king, you got this," D'Anthony assured, giving his youngest brother a pat on the back. He stashed the knapsack of money in a hidden spot he was sure no one would find. From his closet, he retrieved a sandwich bag filled with pretty green nuggets covered in purple crystals. Locking the bedroom door, he plopped down on his little brother's bunk, busted a blunt open, emptied its guts, and started rolling up.

"Yeah, baby, that's what I'm talkin' about!" Jericho yelled, scoring a touchdown.

"See there? Big bruh told you," D'Anthony cracked a grin.

"Man, please, that's one touchdown. The game is far from over." Terrio chimed in.

"Don't forget to use the play-action pass," D'Anthony advised one of his brothers, who was struggling with the game. "It'll keep the defense guessing."

Tucking the freshly rolled blunt behind his ear, D'Anthony walked out of the room. As he crossed the open door of his mother's bedroom, he saw her kneeling beside her bed, praying for him. "God, please forgive my baby for whatever he has done to get his hands on this dirty money..."

D'Anthony shook his head, thinking, *Ma, have you ever stopped to think that maybe it was God that put me in the right circumstances to be able to get my hands on this schmoney? This may have been The Almighty's plan for all we know. Dead that though. I'll be damned if I apologize for gettin' a bag.*

CHAPTER SIXTEEN

D'Anthony continued out the front door, entering the hallway where his four homies were waiting.

"Yo, let's get some pizza and wings," one of them suggested. "And invite some hoodrats over to my place."

D'Anthony grinned, feeling the adrenaline rush of his newfound position. "That's what's up. Let's make it happen."

Marlo clapped him on the back. "It's been a minute since we had a night like this, gang. Feels good to have you back."

"Feels good to be back," D'Anthony replied. "But remember, this is just the beginning. We gotta lotta work ahead of us if we're gonna take over Brooklyn."

Jay nodded, his eyes gleaming with excitement. "We're ready, D. Just say the word."

As they walked down the hallway, D'Anthony's mind raced with thoughts of the future. He was ready to take on the world, and with his crew by his side, nothing could stop him. They made their way to Marlo's apartment, already planning the night's festivities.

"Yo, Marlo, order that pizza and wings. Get the good shit," D'Anthony said, pulling out his phone to send a quick text. "And I'll take care of the hoes."

"You got it, boss," Marlo said, dialing the local Pizza Hut. "This is gonna be a night to remember."

***

The group settled into Marlo's apartment, the smell of pizza and wings soon filling the air. They laughed and joked, the room buzzing with energy. As the night went on, the hoodrats arrived, and the party kicked into high gear.

D'Anthony pulled his crew aside, lowering his voice. "Listen up. We're celebrating tonight, but come tomorrow, it's time to get serious. We need to establish our presence and start making moves."

"We got your back, D'Anthony," Marcus said, his tone sober. "Whatever you need."

D'Anthony nodded, feeling the weight of leadership settle on his shoulders. "Good. Because this is our time. And we're gonna take it, one block at a time."

As D'Anthony looked around at his crew, he knew they were ready for the challenges ahead. Together, they would rise, and Brooklyn would be theirs.

A couple of days later

King Morpheus slipped on his gloves, the well-worn leather fitting snugly over his fingers. The morning sun cast long shadows across the yard, and the air was filled with the sound of clinking weights and grunts of exertion. This was his sanctuary, where he could focus his mind and strengthen his body. He began his stretching routine, feeling the familiar pull of his muscles as they loosened.

King Morpheus was halfway through his stretches when two men approached him, putting on their gloves. The first was King Yak, a brown-skinned man with meticulously groomed 360-waves, goatee, and bifocals. Despite his slim frame, his body was chiseled with defined muscles. His serious demeanor and sharp intellect made him formidable within the Kings of Thieves.

Beside him was King Shyne, a stark contrast in build and appearance. He was larger and more muscular, King Shyne's mixed heritage of Puerto Rican and African American gave him a distinctive look. His head was shaved on the sides, and his hair was styled in two braids that hung over his forehead, giving him an almost warrior-like appearance.

"Morning, Morpheus," King Yak said, adjusting his glasses as he flexed his arms.

"Top of the A.M., Yak. Shyne," Morpheus replied with a nod.

King Shyne grinned, his white teeth flashing against his dark skin. "Ready to get this workout in, king?"

"Always," Morpheus returned the smile. "Let's start with some shadowboxing to warm up."

The three men moved into position, their bodies shifting fluidly as they began to shadowbox. The movements were precise and controlled, a testament to their discipline and training. After a few minutes, Morpheus paused, signaling for a break. He wiped the sweat from his brow and turned to his comrades. "I've got something to tell y'all."

King Yak and King Shyne looked at him expectantly.

"I'll be leaving tomorrow to attend my brother's funeral," Morpheus said, his voice heavy with emotion.

Both men stopped their movements, expressions of sympathy crossing their faces. "Sorry for yo' loss, King," King Yak said sincerely.

"Yeah, King," King Shyne added, placing a supportive hand on Morpheus's shoulder. "My condolences. Dolph was a good man."

Morpheus nodded, appreciating their words. "Thanks, brothers. That means a lot."

Yak frowned, concern etched across his face. "You know who did it?"

Morpheus's eyes hardened. "Notta clue," he admitted, his voice filled with sorrow. "But I swear, I'm gonna find out. And whoever did this is gonna pay me in flesh and blood."

Shyne nodded firmly. "We're with you, King. Anything you need, just say the word."

With a silent agreement, the men resumed their workout. The atmosphere was charged with a mix of camaraderie and resolve. They pushed each other harder, their shared grief translating into raw energy and power.

"You've always got our support," Yak said between punches. "We'll hold things down here while you're gone."

Morpheus ducked a jab and countered with a swift uppercut. "I know you will. We've got to stay strong, stay united."

Shyne, dodging a quick series of blows, added, "We'll keep an ear to the ground, and see if we can dig up any leads on who might be responsible for Dolph's death."

Morpheus nodded, feeling the burn in his muscles as he moved. "Good. This isn't just about me. It's about all of us. Dolph's murder affects the whole kingdom."

As they finished their vigorous workout, all three men were drenched in sweat but fueled by a shared sense of purpose. They removed their gloves, the morning sun now higher in the sky.

"We'll find 'em, Morpheus," Yak said, his voice steady. "And when we do, they'll regret ever crossing The Kings of Thieves."

"Count on it," Shyne added.

Morpheus felt a renewed sense of purpose and solidarity. There were many challenges ahead, but with leaders like Yak and Shyne by his side, he knew the Kings of Thieves would remain solid. He looked at his brothers, the weight of his vow hanging in the air. "Appreciate y'all, word is bond."

***

After they finished their workout, the three leaders gathered by the benches, taking a moment to hydrate and cool down.

"Morpheus," Yak began, "you need anything for the funeral? Any arrangements we can help with?"

Morpheus took a deep breath, wiping sweat from his forehead. "I've got most of it covered. Just needa make sure security is tight. I don't want any surprises while we're paying our respects."

Shyne nodded. "We'll have our best men there. No one gets in without yo' say-so."

Morpheus appreciated the offer. "I trust you both. This is more than just a funeral. It's a statement. We need to show everyone that we're still strong, still united."

Yak adjusted his glasses, his expression thoughtful. "Do you think Dolph's killers will make a move during the funeral?"

Morpheus's eyes narrowed. "They'd be foolish to try. But we can't rule anything out. Stay vigilant. I want everyone on high alert."

Shyne leaned in, his voice low. "And what about after the funeral? Any plans for how we're gonna start looking for who did this?"

Morpheus clenched his fists, the leather gloves creaking. "I've got that faded."

The three men fell silent for a moment, each lost in their thoughts. The loss of Dolph was a heavy blow, but it also solidified their resolve. They were a family, bound by more than just loyalty—they were bound by blood, sweat, and shared history.

"We'll get through this," Morpheus said finally, voice firm. "For Dolph."

Yak and Shyne echoed his sentiment. "For Dolph."

With a final nod, they rose from the benches, their minds set on the tasks ahead. As they walked back toward the main building, the resolve to find justice for Dolph burning brightly within them, they knew that whatever challenges lay ahead, they would face them together.

***

The rest of the day was spent preparing for Morpheus's departure. He coordinated with Yak and Shyne, ensuring that all operations would run smoothly in his absence. As evening fell, the three men gathered one last time in the common area.

"Tomorrow's a big day," Morpheus said, looking at his brothers. "Keep everything tight. I'll be back soon."

"Safe travels, Morpheus," Yak said, giving him a firm handshake.

"Take care, my nigga," Shyne added, pulling him into a brief hug.

Morpheus nodded, a small smile playing on his lips. "I will. And when I get back, we'll find the bastards who did this."

As he walked back to his cell, Morpheus felt a sense of determination and resolve. The Kings of Thieves were more than just a gang—they were his family. And he would do whatever it took to protect them and avenge his brother's death.

***

The prison van rolled to a stop with a creaky groan, its engine rumbling like a caged beast. King Morpheus peered through the barred window, taking in the scene outside. The road to the cemetery was lined with vehicles painted in the unmistakable hues of purple and gold. An army of male and female Kings of Thieves members stood at attention, their eyes burning with the fierce loyalty and grief that united them at this moment—seeing the organization he, King Yak, and King Shyne had built brought a smirk to his lips. It was crazy to him how they started as three, but now they were a few thousand strong. He had enough soldiers and guns to declare war on a small country.

King Morpheus stepped out of the van, his movements restricted by the heavy shackles clamped around his wrists and ankles. The clanking of chains was a stark reminder of his captivity, yet his presence was anything but subdued. Officers with K.O.T ties flanked him, their expressions hard and respectful.

As he approached Dolph's gravesite, the crowd parted like the Red Sea. He kissed a red rose, the petals soft against his lips, and held it above the grave for a moment, eyes closed in silent prayer. Then with a swift motion, he tossed it into the six-foot-deep hole where Dolph's coffin lay.

"Rest easy, baby bro," he murmured, his voice thick with emotion. "I swear on my life, I'll get revenge for you."

***

On his way out of the cemetery, a figure emerged from the crowd and approached King Morpheus. Chyna, face set in a mask of seriousness, extended his hand. The two men shook hands, a silent exchange of humility and respect.

"Chyna," King Morpheus began, his voice steady despite the turmoil within, "I need you to lead the Kings of Thieves now that Dolph is gone."

Chyna's eyes widened slightly, the gravity of the request sinking in. "Me? I...I don't know if I'm ready yet."

"You are," King Morpheus said firmly. "Dolph spoke very highly of you. You've got what it takes. I'ma have a cell phone and some bread delivered to you. The celly is to be used to contact me, and that's it."

Chyna nodded slowly, still processing. "Hold up. How are you gon' know where to drop off everythang? I didn't give you my addy."

King Morpheus's lips curved into a knowing smile. "I have eyes and ears everywhere, Chyna.."

As King Morpheus was being escorted back to the prison van, he nearly collided with a young man who stepped into his path. "My bad, gang," the young man said, extending his hand. "I'm King D. I admire and respect your gangsta. I swear, niggaz gon' get theirs and then some for what they did to yo' bro. That's my word."

King Morpheus took D'Anthony's hand, feeling the sincerity in his grip. "I appreciate that, King. Stay strong and keep your wits about chu."

There's something about that kid...I'm picking up a strange energy from him. Gotta have one of the soldiers do some digging. You can never be too sure of anyone these days, King Morpheus thought as he was escorted back to the prison van.

CHAPTER SEVENTEEN

King Morpheus stared out the window of the prison van, watching the purple and gold-clad figures grow smaller as the vehicle pulled away. The weight of the day pressed heavily on his shoulders. Losing Dolph had been devastating, but he couldn't afford to dwell on it. The future of the Kings of Thieves depended on his leadership, decisions, and ability to see through the murky waters of betrayal and loyalty.

King Morpheus's thoughts drifted to D'Anthony, the eager recruit. There was something about the kid that didn't sit right with him. He knew better than to ignore his instincts. He'd survived this long in the game by trusting his gut, and right now, it was telling him to be cautious.

King Morpheus sighed as he laid his head back, the chains around his wrists clinking softly. "Dolph, wherever you are, be it Heaven or Hell, watch over us. Guide us. We're going to need all the help we can get down here."

As the van drove towards the prison, King Morpheus's mind was already working on the next steps. Revenge for Dolph, maintaining order within the gang, and unraveling the mystery that was D'Anthony. The road ahead was fraught with danger, but he was ready. He had to be.

The Kings of Thieves depended on him, and he wouldn't let them down.

***

Draco sat at the visiting room table waiting for his cousin to arrive. The sterile smell of disinfectant hung in the air, mingling with the faint scent of sweat and despair. He heard the faint buzz of the door opening and watched Shorty walk in, his face lighting up with a smile when he saw Draco. They greeted each other with a dap and a brotherly hug, the brief moment of contact was a rare comfort in the harsh environment.

"Good to see you, bro," Shorty said, stepping back. "You need anything from the vending machines? I saw some decent snacks on my way over here."

"Nah, I'm good," Draco replied, shaking his head. "Let's get down to business."

Draco's eyes sharpened as he leaned forward, lowering his voice. "Did you make sure Berrios got his payment for standing watch over the moreno's father?"

Shorty nodded. "Yeah, he got his cut. I made sure Jorge's funeral expenses were covered too, and laid some cash on his mother so she wouldn't have to worry about working for a while."

"Good," Draco said, a hint of relief in his voice. "And the crew? Have they been taken care of?"

"Yeah, they're okay," Shorty assured him. "I paid them and took care of the connect for another shipment of drugs. Everything's moving smoothly."

Draco's expression softened slightly. "I told you I could hold it down in these streets while you're on this lil' iron vacation, Papi. I got chu."

Draco nodded, appreciating the loyalty. "I can't front, my G. I'm actually impressed by how you're handling business. Salute." He saluted Shorty like a private in the military, and Shorty returned the gesture with a grin.

Draco and Shorty talked a while longer, discussing the latest happenings in the streets. Who got shot, who got locked up, who's messing around with who, and which hood rat was pregnant now?

"You hear about Enrique?" Shorty asked, leaning in closer.

"Nah, what happened?"

"Got locked up last night. Cops caught him with a trunk full of dope. He ain't talking, though."

Draco sighed. "Enrique's a real one. Hopefully, he holds it down."

"And you know Shayla?" Shorty continued. "Turns out she's pregnant again. This makes baby number eight. She needs to slow down."

Draco chuckled, shaking his head. "She never learns. Always chasing the wrong guys."

"Yo, I almost forgot," Shorty said suddenly, his eyes widening. "There's this fight tournament going down in Bali. Everybody's talking about it – barbershops, beauty salons, pickup games, parties, you name it."

Draco leaned back, a wistful look crossing his face. "Man, I wish I was home to catch a flight to Bali. Sounds like it's gonna be lit."

Shorty nodded enthusiastically. "For real. They say some of the best fighters in the world are gonna be there. It's all anyone can talk about."

Draco's eyes sparkled with interest. "Keep me updated on that. If it's as big as you say, it could be an opportunity for us to make some moves."

Before they knew it, one of the corrections officers announced over the loudspeaker that visiting hours were over. The moment of normalcy was coming to an end.

"Gotta go, primo," Draco said, standing up.

Shorty stood after him, giving Draco another hug. "Take care, bro. I'll keep everything running smoothly til you come home."

"I know you will," Draco replied, a rare smile touching his lips. "Stay dangerous."

"You too, primo," Shorty said, walking away as the door buzzed open again.

Draco watched him leave, the door closing with a heavy thud behind him. As he turned to walk back to his cell, the weight of the jail settled back onto his shoulders. But for a brief moment, he had felt a connection to the outside world, a reminder of the life that waited for him beyond the walls.

***

King Morpheus walked back to his cell, wearing a face of practiced indifference. The familiar, dehumanizing process of stripping and being thoroughly searched by correction officers was a routine he had begrudgingly accepted. The cold metal of the handcuffs had left faint red marks on his wrists, a silent testament to the authority that ruled within the prison walls.

The clanging of the cell doors, the shuffling of feet, and the occasional barked orders from corrections officers created a cacophony that King Morpheus had long since learned to tune out. He waltzed through the corridors of the general population unit with the ease of someone who knew every twist and turn, every potential threat and hiding spot.

***

As Draco moved through the passageways, he exchanged nods and brief greetings with his comrades. Each nod was a silent acknowledgment of shared struggles and unspoken alliances.

"Yo, Draco!" A voice called out, and Draco turned to see Alano, a tall, muscular man with a shaved head and a tattoo snaking down his neck.

"Alano," Draco acknowledged with a curt nod. "Everything good?"

"Same old," Alano replied, shrugging. "You know how it is. Heard you got the special treatment again."

Draco smirked. "Yeah, they can't get enough of me."

They shared a brief chuckle before parting ways. Draco's eyes flicked around, taking in the faces of those who stood by him in this concrete jungle. They were a motley crew, bound together by a mutual understanding of survival in this unforgiving environment.

Unbeknownst to them and Draco, the Kings of Thieves would have an agenda, one that would soon bring them into direct conflict. The crazy part about it was that neither party knew they'd clash in the future.

***

Down in the common area, the Kings of Thieves members were engaged in their usual activities. Groups of men huddled around tables, engrossed in games of Spades and Dominoes. Laughter and shouts of triumph punctuated the otherwise monotonous hum of prison life. Others lounged on benches, shooting the breeze and sharing stories.

"Kid, you see that new C.O.? Shorty bad as my two-year-old son," one of the men, a burly figure with a scar across his cheek, said, slapping a domino down on the table. "You can tell she's fresh outta the academy, she's green as a head of cabbage. I'ma bag that, my word is bond."

"Yeah? Well, you willin' to make a lil' wager on that?" Another man asked, with a gap-tooth grin. "'Cause I got two soups and a Snicker that says you don't have a shot."

"Son, you ain't talkin' 'bout nothin', bet." the first man shook hands with the other.

***

King Morpheus's journey back to his cell was merely the prelude to a larger conflict, a silent march towards an inevitable confrontation that would test the limits of their resilience and resolve. Once he reached his cell, he subtly signaled two trusted lieutenants, Preacher and Mook. Both men, who had been playing cards nearby, nodded and sauntered over.

"Preacher, Mook, I need you to watch my back," King Morpheus said quietly, eyes scanning the surroundings. "Make sure no one comes snooping around."

Preacher nodded, taking his position near the entrance to King Morpheus's cell, while Mook positioned himself down the corridor.

With his lookouts in place, King Morpheus retrieved his contraband cellphone from its hiding spot — a loose brick in the wall behind his bunk. He glanced around once more before dialing a familiar number.

The phone rang twice before a young lady picked up, "Hello?"

"'Sup, ma?" King Morpheus said, keeping his voice low. "Listen, I need you to do something for me."

"Anything, bae. What chu need?"

"I need you to drop off a cellphone to the lil' homie Chyna. You know the spot."

"Yeah. I remember it. Is there anythang else?" She asked.

King Morpheus paused, his face forming a scowl. "I need you to have my lil' man put $100,000 onna streets. It's up for grabs for anyone who can deliver baby bro's killerz. I want every corner, every block, every city of every borough turned on its head. Got it?"

There was a brief silence on the other end of the line. "I gotchu, but $100,000 issa big bag. You sure you wanna put out that kinda-"

"I don't give a fuck about that bread, Lawaun," he said, his voice tight with controlled anger. "I needa know who tightened 'em up my kid brother. And I need to know like yesterday, ya dig?"

"A'ight. A'ight. A'ight. I'll get right onnit. Stay dangerous in there."

"Always," King Morpheus replied before disconnecting the call and carefully stashing the phone back in its hiding place. He leaned back against the cold concrete wall of his cell, his brain racing with plans and contingencies. He knew the prison was a powder keg ready to explode, and the upcoming clash with The Kings of Thieves was only a matter of time. But for now, he had done what he could. All that remained was to wait and see who would make the first move.

As he glanced towards the cell door, he saw Preacher and Mook still standing guard, their postures tense and alert. King Morpheus knew he could count on them and the rest of the Kings when the time came. The prison might be a brutal, unforgiving place, but he had built an army that was willing to kill and die on his orders.

CHAPTER EIGHTEEN

Draco walked back inside his cell and recovered his cellphone. He didn't bother having one of the homies lookout for corrections officers, because the ones on this shift were on his payroll. Leaning against the bunk with one arm folded across his chest, he dialed a number and listened to the phone ring.

As soon as the line connected, he began speaking in Spanish. "Mano, how is our friend? Good. Good," Draco nodded, voice calm and controlled. "Oh, no. Everything is excellent. I was just calling to check in on the Goose that laid the Golden Egg. Listen, Shorty came to see me, he said he dropped that package on you."

"Yes. I got it. Thanks again," came the reply.

"No need to thank me, bro. You earned every penny."

"Still, you put me in position, Manny. With the bills piling up and my son needing this surgery, that blessing came right on time."

"Understood," Draco replied, his tone softening slightly. "Look, I've gotta go, we'll talk again soon."

"Okay. Take care."

***

Berrios, Trick's nurse, sat on the toilet in a men's room stall. He'd just hung up with Draco and laid his head back against the wall, taking a deep breath. He hated the situation he was in but he didn't have a choice. He agreed to take a bag from Draco to pay his bills because if he didn't, not only would his family end up on the streets, he wouldn't be able to pay for his son's heart surgery. Without the money for the operation, he was sure he and his fiancée would be planning their son's funeral, something neither of them was ready to face.

Pocketing his cellphone, Berrios walked out of the stall and splashed water on his face. Grasping the porcelain sink on either side, he stared at his reflection, watching water slide down his face and drip off his chin. Snatching a few paper towels from the dispenser, he dried his face and hands and left the men's room. He forced a smile onto his face, hiding the stress and turmoil he was dealing with internally.

Berrios grinned and nodded at the cop posted outside Trick's room door. "Here to give my guy his sponge bath," he said, voice steady. The cop nodded understandingly.

Entering the room, Berrios donned latex gloves and carried a basin of hot, sudsy water. Although Trick was in a coma, Berrios made small talk, believing that he could hear him.

As he washed Trick's arm, Berrios couldn't help but glance at the four ink pens in the pocket of his scrubs top. One of them was a syringe filled with cyanide, capable of killing a man almost instantly. Ever since he'd accepted the cash for the job, he had been praying he wouldn't get the call to administer the lethal injection. He wasn't sure he could go through with killing someone, but he was positive that if he didn't, he'd be putting his and his family's life in jeopardy.

"I don't know what kinda crap you've gotten yourself mixed up in, unc," Berrios said under his breath, washing Trick's arm. "But I hope for both our sakes Draco never makes that call."

Berrios continued the sponge bath, his mind filled with thoughts of his son and the precarious situation he was in. The minutes dragged on, each filled with an overwhelming sense of dread. He hoped and prayed that he wouldn't have to choose between his moral compass and the livelihood of his family.

As he finished, he carefully placed the basin back on the counter and removed his gloves, throwing them in the trash. He took a deep breath and stepped out of the room, nodding again to the cop outside.

Berrios walked down the corridor, his heart heavy with the weight of his actions and the fear of what might come next.

***

The gang sat at the kitchen table enjoying the delicious breakfast Chrissy whipped up that morning. The boys were asleep until the smell of buttermilk pancakes, crisp bacon, eggs, and hash teased their empty bellies. Before Chrissy could head upstairs to wake everyone to eat they were already marching into the kitchen, looking to satisfy their hunger.

While Jayvon, Chrissy, Augustus, and Bag Man were discussing the baby, Chyna was scrolling through his call log to see if he'd missed a call from this baddie he bagged a couple of days ago. His forehead wrinkled when he noticed an unexpected call to D'Anthony on the night they discussed the Finesse lick. He didn't remember speaking to him, yet the call log showed he was on the line for 45 minutes. Realization struck him like the hand of a scorned lover—D'Anthony had been involved in jacking them for the money they stole from Finesse.

Chyna's frustration boiled over, and he cursed loudly. "Disloyal, bitch ass, punk muthafucka!"

Jayvon, Chrissy, Bag Man, and Augustus looked up, alarmed by Chyna's outburst. "What's wrong, bro?" Jayvon asked, concern plastered on his face.

Chyna's eyes blazed with anger as he turned to face them, his voice a growl. "I know who hit us for the money we stole from Finesse," he spat.

A wave of shock and fury washed over the room. Chrissy's mouth fell open, Bag Man shook his head, and Augustus clenched his fists, knuckles turning white.

"Who?" Augustus demanded, voice trembling with anger.

"That goddamn D'Anthony," Chyna hissed. "I called 'em that night, but I don't remember talking to him. He hadda heard us discussing the lick."

Without wasting another second, Chyna dialed D'Anthony's number, his hands shaking with rage. The phone rang twice before D'Anthony answered.

"Yo, what's up, Chyna?" D'Anthony said casually.

Chyna's voice was ice-cold, barely contained fury simmering beneath the surface. "I know what you did, you fuckin' Judas. You think you can play us and get away with it?" There was a tense silence on the other end of the line. The room seemed to hold its breath as they awaited D'Anthony's response.

"Man, I don't know what you're talking about," D'Anthony replied, tone defensive but with an edge of nervousness.

"Don't play dumb with me," Chyna snapped. "I know you were in onna heist. You're gonna pay for this."

The silence on the other end was deafening. Jayvon, Chrissy, Bag Man, and Augustus watched Chyna intently, their expressions a mix of anger and anticipation.

"You better watch your back, lil' nigga," Chyna warned, disconnecting the call, and leaving the air in the room crackling with tension.

Jayvon placed a hand on Chyna's shoulder, his expression grim. "We'll deal with 'em."

Bag Man and Augustus echoed their agreement, their expressions hardening. The betrayal had stung deep, but they were ready to strike back. They had been wronged, and now it was time for retribution.

"You fuckin' right we are," Chyna replied, heading out of the kitchen.

"Where are you going?" Jayvon asked.

Chyna stopped at the doorway, turning around. "I'm finna get the sticks. I know where ol' boy is, but he doesn't know that I know."

"Hold up. I'ma roll witchu," Bag Man ate the last of his eggs. He snatched the napkin out of his collar and followed Chyna out of the kitchen.

"No way I'm gonna miss out on gettin' in on the action," Augustus finished his cup of coffee and followed Bag Man and Chyna out of the kitchen.

Chrissy looked at Jayvon. "Lemme guess, you're gonna go with them?"

Jayvon shook his head and grasped her hand. "Nah. The king's gonna stay behind and watch after his queen, this time." he kissed her forehead.

CHAPTER NINETEEN

The shit had hit the fan at Bartise's spot, leaving Finesse with hefty attorney fees, and even worse, his question unanswered—Where the fuck was Chrissy? Finesse was under immense stress, and began to become depressed. The only thing that seemed to help when he was in this state of mind was money, since he didn't have much of that, he opted for the next best thing—pussy.

Finesse lay asleep in bed between two beautiful Brazilian women with tan lines. The sunlight shined on his face causing him to frown and flutter his eyelids. He looked around trying to figure out where he was. He'd spent most of the night having sex, drinking, and doing every party drug one could imagine. Coming to the realization where he was, Finesse stretched his arms above his head and yawned. Scratching his hairy chest, he looked at the beauty lying asleep to his left and made note of the cocaine residue on her ass cheek. Reaching over her, he picked up the rolled-up hundred-dollar bill from his nightstand and used it to snort what was left of the powder. He threw his head back, making funny noises with his nose and mouth. He then smacked the girl lying asleep on his left on her buttocks and slid out of bed. He tied his robe around his waist and took the elevator to the first floor. Entering his kitchen, he was approached by his butler who had a cup of coffee and a newspaper. He thanked the servant and sat at the kitchen table, sipping his hot beverage and reading over the paper.

The doorbell ringing resonated throughout the house.

"I'll get it, sir," the butler told Finesse as he walked out of the kitchen.

Finesse went on reading his newspaper and sipping his coffee like he hadn't heard him. Shortly, the butler returned with a gold envelope he'd signed for at the door. He extended the envelope to Finesse who looked at it like what the fuck is this? The butler picked up on his expression and shrugged. After sitting down the coffee and newspaper on the table, Finesse took the envelope from his servant and went back to sweeping. Finesse noticed the envelope didn't have the sender's address so he was curious as to where it had come from. He didn't waste a second longer before he tore the envelope open and read over the gold invitation inside of it. The invitation was to a fight tournament in Bali. Finesse massaged his chin as he thought about a night out of the country. He didn't have shit popping on the night of the fights so he was looking for something to get into.

I think I will hop on a flight and shoot over to Bali. I could use something to keep my mind off the gwap those black bitchez stole from me, but once my lil' retreat is over, I'm back on the hunt.

"Roderick," Finesse called for his butler. The old Black man with the white cotton hair and goatee appeared at his side like a magic trick.

"Yes, sir," Roderick asked, holding the broom and dustpan.

"Call Ennis and have 'em bring the car around. I want him to drop off last night's entertainment."

"I'll get on it right away, sir."

"Then I'd like you to pack a week's worth of underwear and only the best of my suits." Finesse told him. "I'll be catching a flight out of state to a special event, and I'd like to be dressed to the 9's when I grace those in attendance with my presence."

"Consider it done, sir," Roderick said, returning the broom and dustpan to its rightful place.

Finesse laid back in his chair sipping from his hot cup, thinking about the blast he was going to have in Bali.

***

Chrissy picked up the invitation and studied it closely. "So, you're really gonna go through with this, huh?" she shifted her glassy pink eyes to Jayvon. He'd just told her he was entering Bartise's fight tournament in Bali for a chance to win the prize money.

Jayvon nodded. "No doubt. This is the only way I see myself getting this bag so these fools won't tighten up my pops."

"But you said—"

"I know what I told you, but my back is against the wall, Doll."

"Von, we've gotta baby on the way, you've gotta family to think about."

"I am thinking about my family," he assured her, "my old man is my family."

Chrissy had known Jayvon long enough to know that once he had his mind made up on something there wasn't any way someone could change it. At this point, she could only support him and hope for the best.

Chrissy crawled over to Jayvon straddling his waist and slipping her arms around his neck. He ran his hands up and down her back soothingly. He then kissed her twice on the side of her face. He could tell by the way she was breathing she was still crying.

"I love you, Doll," Jayvon told her.

Sniffling, Chrissy took the time to get herself together before responding to him. "I—I love you, too."

There was a silence that seemed to last for an eternity.

"Promise me something."

"Anything, boo."

"Promise me you're gonna win this thing."

"I promise. I got this shit in the bag."

Jayvon wiped the wetness from her eyes and kissed her.

"Take me upstairs and make love to me."

"I gotchu," Jayvon replied. She held on to him as he rose from the couch and carried her upstairs to their bedroom.

***

D'Anthony telling his homies that they were going to get down to business after the little shindig at Marlo's crib was bullshit. They'd spent the past couple of days shopping, partying, and fucking like judgment day was approaching. Every time he brought up getting the ball rolling the fellas would protest for one more day, and he'd give in, but he promised himself that last night would be his last day of partying and bullshit. So whoever wasn't trying to make the moves he had lined up to put them on top could get the fuck on. It was time to get serious.

Half-naked women and men lie asleep, sprawled about the living room. Among them were bottles of alcohol, styrofoam cups, empty pizza boxes, and black containers with buffalo wing bones on the coffee table, floor, and kitchen counter. D'Anthony and his boys partied like rockstars and fucked their female guests like they were groupies.

While Marlo and Grant had the living room sewn up, D'Anthony lies in the bedroom under a pile of arms and legs of three young women. Hearing his cellphone ringing and vibrating, D'Anthony began to stir awake. Yawning, he looked around for his cell, but he didn't see it anywhere. Realizing it was under one of the broads he'd crushed last night, he rolled her over and retrieved it. D'Anthony looked at his cellular's screen, it was Chyna hitting him up. He didn't know if he was calling on some social shit, or if he suspected him of jacking his lick.

"Whaddup, big bro?" D'Anthony asked, rubbing his eye.

"Don't whaddup big bro me, lil' muthafucka," Chyna snarled, voice dripping with anger. "I know it was you, and most likely that bitch ass nigga Bocka, that finagled us outta that jux."

D'Anthony played dumb. "What? Fuck you talkin' about, gang?" he asked, fishing what was left of a blunt. He took the time to light it up while listening to Chyna.

"I'm talking about putting a bullet in yo' ass, Gump," Chyna threatened before abruptly disconnecting the call.

D'Anthony's heart raced as he stared at his cellphone, the weight of Chyna's threat sinking into his brain. He knew it was on between him and Chyna now. The good thing was he only had to worry about Jayvon, Augustus, and Bag Man. They'd be backing up Chyna, no doubt. The Kings of Thieves wouldn't lend him a hand because the lick he'd hit wasn't sanctioned.

D'Anthony placed a call to Jay. "'Sup, my nigga, y'all on the way to The Chi with my fam yet?"

"Shit, gang, we're on the highway now," Jay replied.

"Cool. You and Hill keep yo' eyes peeled, I just gotta call from son I was tellin' y'all about."

"Say no mo', my nig, ya boy's head stay onna swivel, ya dig?"

"No doubt. Love, fool."

"Love, my G." Jay disconnected the call.

D'Anthony laid his head back against the headboard and sat his cellular on his stomach. The blunt pinched between his finger and thumb burned down to a stub, having been forgotten during his conversation with Chyna. There wasn't any doubt in his mind that he had to peel Chyna and his people's onions now. Slaying Jayvon and the others wouldn't phase D'Anthony mentally, but putting his gun on Chyna was something different. He loved that nigga like he was one of his siblings so drilling him would be like killing one of them.

Chyna wasn't one to make empty threats. The man was dangerous and had a reputation for letting his gun blow, especially when he felt like a nigga played him. D'Anthony's thoughts were a whirlwind of potential plans and precautions. He needed to be ready for whatever Chyna might throw his way.

"Thank you. I'll never, ever forget what you've done for me and mine. I love you, big bruh, no cap."

"I love you too, B. We are family so I'ma always hold you down."

"Vise versa. Loyalty."

D'Anthony looked down at the "Loyalty" tattoo across his stomach in Old English letters. Unconsciously, he rubbed his fingers across it, thinking of how he was a disloyal ass nigga that didn't have any business getting the word inked on his skin. He let his head fall back against the headboard and expelled air.

Shit's fucked up, but I'm waist-deep innit now. It's too late to turn back.

***

Chyna, Bag Man, and Augustus pulled ski masks over their faces, adjusting them until they could see out of the eye holes properly. They slid on black sunglasses, the dark lenses reflecting their steely determination. Picking up their M-16 assault rifles, they stood silently, watching the numbers above the elevator doors light up one by one, each ding a step closer to their target. When the elevator reached D'Anthony's floor, the doors slid open with a soft chime. Without hesitation, they stepped out, their footsteps echoing in unison as they speed-walked down the corridor. Their hearts pounded in their chests, adrenaline sharpening their focus.

They approached the apartment, a singular purpose driving them forward.

***

D'Anthony and his friends were cleaning up the remnants of the previous night's party, laughing and joking, oblivious to the impending danger. The sound of crumpling cans and muffled conversations filled the room, masking the threat drawing near. The door burst open with a thunderous crash, splintering wood and shattering their peace. Chyna, Bag Man, and Augustus rushed in, their rifles raised.

To Be Continued...

BLOODY KNUCKLES 3

My self-published books

BLOODY KNUCKLES
THE DEVIL WEARS TIMBS 1-7
ME AND MY HITTAZ 1-6
THE LAST REAL NIGGA ALIVE 1-3
A HOOD NIGGA'S BLUES
A SOUTH CENTRAL LOVE AFFAIR

My books published under LDP

BURY ME A G 1-5
THE DOPEMAN'S BODYGUARD 1-2
FEAR MY GANGSTA 1-5
THESE SCANDALOUS STREETS 1-3
THE REALEST KILLAZ 1-3
THE LAST OF THE OG'S 1-3
A GANGSTA'S EMPIRE 1-4
GOD BLESS THE TRAPPERS 1-3

Coming Soon

BLOODY KNUCKLES 2
THERE'S NO PLACE IN HEAVEN FOR THUGS
THEY MADE ME AN ANIMAL

www.ingramcontent.com/pod-product-compliance
Lightning Source LLC
LaVergne TN
LVHW021817060526
838201LV00058B/3420